MURDER IN G MAJOR

Ziggy Gertner

P. L. Gertner

P. L. Gertner
Visit my website at www.gertnermedia.com

Printed in the United States of America
First Printing: April 2020

Independently Published
ISBN - 9798634274058

Other Books by P. L. Gertner

Caryn O'Neal Series

A Trace of Treachery (Book 1)
Tangled Two-Step (Book 2)
Another Pretty Face (Book 3)

Ellie Nelson Series

A Key to Murder (Book 1)
Canvas for Murder (Book 2)
Casting Call for Murder (Book 3)
Plein Air Murder (Book 4)

Claire Olson Series
(in collaboration with D. P. Gertner)

Elementary, My Dear (Book 1)

CHAPTER 1

Gessie Chapel went into a closing riff on her guitar as she sang the final words to "Jolene." The couple who had requested the song dropped what looked to be a $10 bill into the crown of her cowboy hat, which was upended and sitting in the middle of her guitar case for just such a purpose. She nodded her thanks and decided she was through for the day. As the couple walked away, Gessie emptied the money out of the crown of her cowboy hat. She stuffed the money in the center compartment of her guitar case and set the hat atop her head. She had just laid her guitar inside the case and snapped the latches shut when two men stepped in front of her.

Twilight was fast fading, but the streetlights along 2nd Avenue were already on, and they, combined with the neon signs of the storefronts and eateries, provided enough light for Gessie to see the two men in front of her were going to be trouble. One was a big barrel-chested man Gessie figured to be in his forties. He might have been fit at one time, maybe even an athlete. But most of the muscle had turned to flab, and the broken blood vessels visible on his cheeks clearly indicated the man liked to drink, and often. His sidekick--Gessie was sure that was what the other man was--looked to be about the same age, but was much smaller in stature. Gessie would have bet money the two had been friends since their high school days. The big man had probably been the star of the football team, and the little man probably followed him around like a puppy dog, happy for the attention, and doing anything the big man wanted him to do. It looked like that relationship dynamic was still in full force.

"Well, look what we got here, Zack. One of them buskers," the big man said a little too loudly. The words were slightly slurred, and he stumbled a little as he threw an elbow out to nudge his friend like he was going to let him in on some kind of secret or a joke. Zack didn't look any steadier than his buddy, and Gessie had to react quickly to pick her guitar case up and out of the way when the guy looked like he was going to stagger right into the middle of it.

"Come on, darlin', get that guitar back out. Zack here wants to hear a song. Don't you, Zack?"

Zack was bobbing his head up and down, and the movement caused him to stagger a bit more. Gessie thought he would have actually fallen over if the big man hadn't reached out at the last minute and grabbed Zack's arm. Maybe he still had some of his athletic reflexes left after all.

"Sorry, fellas, I'm packing up for the day. I'll be here tomorrow if you want to come back."

"Now, see, that's no good. We'll be leaving tomorrow morning. I know. Let's have a private party. Zack, grab the little lady's guitar, and we'll head on over to the hotel and have some fun."

As the big man had been talking, Gessie had gripped the handle of the guitar case tighter in her left hand and, with her right hand, had reached casually into the back pocket of her jeans where she kept a can of mace. She didn't get hassled often, but there was always a risk performing out on the street, especially in an area full of bars. The streets were usually full of people, and even those with a buzz on were just out to enjoy themselves and take in the vibe of the area and its music. This wasn't one of those times, however. There was no one else close by, and while Zack might have been a happy drunk, his buddy was anything but.

Gessie stood up, continuing to hold her guitar case in front of her with one hand and the mace in the other, hidden slightly behind her back. While it would pain her to have to use the guitar as a weapon, she would do whatever it took if it became necessary. It was a hard-shell case, and she figured it could do some damage if she swung it and connected it with the big guy's knee. The mace could be used on both men, and there were always her cowboy boots. The pointed toe could put either man in a world of hurt if she could land a kick in just the right spot.

"I'm not going anywhere with you. You're drunk. I suggest you both just leave before you get hurt."

The big man laughed. Actually, there wasn't anything funny about the sound he made. It was more guttural and left no doubt in Gessie's mind things were about to turn ugly.

"Oh, she's a feisty one, Zack. Just how I like 'em."

"Yeah, Ray, yeah," Zack answered with a bit of crazy in his voice. Maybe he wasn't as harmless as Gessie had initially thought.

Several things happened at once. The big man started to reach for Gessie, and Gessie flipped off the safety on the top of the mace canister she still held behind her back. She was about to swing her arm out and release a stream of mace, when a voice came from behind the man she now knew was named Ray.

"The lady asked you to leave."

The voice startled Ray. He turned away from Gessie to see who had dared to interrupt him. Whatever words he was going to say died on his lips. While he might have had enough bravado to take on the man who had spoken, three other men were standing just slightly in back of that man.

"Come on, Ray. She ain't worth it," Zach spoke up and tugged on his friend's arm as he looked nervously around. It looked to Gessie like he was ready to bolt and wanted to make sure he had a clear path.

Where the man who had spoken was tall and slender, the three men with him were not. Since she had already been thinking of athletes, Gessie imagined the slender man to be the quarterback, two of the men to be his offensive line, and the third possibly a tight end. These guys looked like Ray might have looked ten years ago. They were younger, and their bodies were still in shape. It didn't take a genius to see Ray was outmatched.

"We were just having some fun," Ray said as he eased away from Gessie, "Didn't mean any harm. Come on, Zack. We got better things to do."

As he was speaking, Ray started backing away slowly. When the four men continued to advance toward him, he turned abruptly and started walking down 2nd Avenue toward Broadway. Zack lost no time as he scrambled to follow his friend.

The four men didn't say anything else. They kept a reasonable distance but casually followed Ray and Zack down the street. Once they were sure the two men weren't going to be any further trouble, the slender man turned back toward where Gessie had been, but she was no longer there.

As soon as Gessie thought the men were far enough away, she had moved quickly to the recessed doorway right next to where she had been playing. Unless you were familiar with the area, you would have no idea the doorway led to an inner courtyard surrounded by several loft apartments created inside an old warehouse. Gessie didn't always perform right outside her own door, but she was glad she had chosen to do so that day.

She hurried to her apartment, set her guitar case down just inside the door, and went straight to the refrigerator where she pulled out a bottle of Yazoo beer. The local brew was just what was needed after being out in the 80-degree heat and then narrowly missing having to deal with a drunk in full mid-life crisis.

As she unscrewed the cap and took a sip of the cold beer, she tried to analyze her feelings about what had just happened. She realized she was angry. Sure. Anyone would be. That Ray guy was a jerk and a drunk jerk at that. But she was ready to handle the situation. And that was when the other man had stepped in. She decided she was a bit angry at him also. That wasn't really his fault. He was probably just being helpful. It didn't mean he thought Gessie was weak and needed a man to protect her, to tell her what to do, what to wear, what...

Gessie stopped herself and took another sip of beer. This time she realized she was angry with herself. She'd moved to Nashville from California to put her previous life behind her. It didn't do her a bit of good if she was going to dredge it all up at the drop of a hat, and lump every guy she met into the same category as her ex.

If she was honest with herself, maybe she was a little scared, too. Surprisingly though, she wasn't afraid of the drunk jerk and his creepy little friend. She still thought she would have handled that situation.

What scared her a bit was her reaction to Joe Quarterback. Because she hadn't stuck around to learn his name, that was how she thought of him. And the fact she was still thinking of him was just ridiculous. It's true he was good looking. He had dark hair and eyes and just enough facial hair that made Gessie wonder if the look was intentional or just the result of a five o'clock shadow. He was wearing a faded White Lightning George Jones Signature T-shirt, jeans, and cowboy boots. She wasn't sure what the other guys looked like because she had been too busy looking at Joe Quarterback.

Their eyes had met for only the briefest of moments. What was it they always said in romance novels? "Her heart fluttered, and her breath caught, as his eyes met hers." Again. Ridiculous. Gessie chugged down the last of the beer, and told herself her heart wasn't racing again at the thought of the tall, slender man. She had sworn off men. She didn't want anything to do with another man, not so soon after Burton. Well, she could put her mind at rest. There was nothing she could do about it anyway. She didn't know the guy's name and would likely never see him again.

CHAPTER 2

essie Chapel had only been in Nashville for a month, and she was still getting the feel of the city as well as her new life. It was a far cry from where she'd been. When Gessie was in elementary school, she had routinely tested high in the standardized science and mathematics tests. It had won her a small scholarship and placement in an advanced math curriculum when she started high school. She was taken under the wing of one of her teachers, who was involved with the STEM program in the Kansas City area. STEM stood for Science, Technology, Engineering, and Mathematics. The goal of the program was to encourage students to pursue careers in those disciplines, especially female students.

Early on, Gessie demonstrated she had uncanny mathematics and computer skills, and she excelled in the advanced STEM classes. As her graduation loomed, it was no surprise to anyone when she was offered a scholarship to Stanford to pursue a joint Computer Science/MBA degree.

It was an accelerated degree program, and once again, Gessie excelled. So much so that she had several job offers waiting for her once she had obtained her masters. With almost no break in between, Gessie went from a full-time student to a full-time employee of a software company in Palo Alto, California.

What had been lost during all this was time for Gessie to pursue her real passion. And that was music. She had been singing since she was a toddler, and that included making up her own songs as she played. Gessie's mother was a country music fan. Some of Gessie's fondest memories were of her and her mother driving to someplace or other, with the radio cranked up and the two of them singing at the top of their lungs.

She had received a guitar for her tenth birthday, and her parents had joked they hadn't seen her for three years after that because she spent every moment she could in her bedroom teaching herself how to play. When she was a freshman in high school, she had entered the school's talent contest and had come in first place with her rendition of Carrie Underwood's "Jesus Take the Wheel."

But soon after that, Gessie found there was less and less time to play her guitar and write her own music. Her studies took up so much of her time; it seemed she only got to play and sing on Sundays. Her church had what they called a guitar mass to attract and involve the younger members of the congregation. Gessie was part of the musical group that led the congregation in the more modern songs for that service.

But she didn't even do that once she graduated and moved to California. Her studies were even more intense. She'd look up from one of her textbooks and sigh when she noticed the layer of dust on her guitar case propped up in the corner of her dorm room.

She'd finished top in her class, and while she had several offers to consider, she had chosen a nearby company called Financial Management Systems. FMS had offered her an outrageous salary, but she found out they expected a lot for their money. She was immediately thrust into a major development project for a new line of software. The project had an unrealistic deadline, and everyone involved had to put in insane amounts of overtime to stay anywhere close to schedule. Gessie was a significant factor in the successful completion of the project, and her star began to rise. She was assigned to the best and most visible projects, and had moved up steadily in the five years she had been with the company.

A year ago, she had come to the attention of the Vice President of Marketing for FMS. Burton Halstead had relocated from the Los Angeles office to Palo Alto, and it seemed he immediately set his sights on Gessie. The rumor going around was the only reason he had moved to the Palo Alto office was that he had already gone through every female in the L.A. office and was looking for new conquests.

Although she had initially turned down his invitations, he had continued to pursue her. He was a few years older than she was, and he seemed very polished. Something you'd expect from the vice president of a major company. He was good-looking, and there hadn't been any recent rumors about him in the Palo Alto office. So, eventually, he had worn her down, and she had agreed to go out on a date with him. Over the course of two months, he had wined her and dined her and really put on the charm. He'd seemed sincere when he'd told Gessie he had changed, and it was all because of her. He'd said she was the only woman for him, and he convinced her to move in with him. Things went fine at first, but Gessie began to realize Burton had a controlling side.

When they weren't at work, Burton decided who they saw, where they ate, what they did. Initially, Gessie didn't mind. She liked most of Burton's choices, at least well enough that it wasn't worth an argument. But that changed when Burton became obsessive with where she was at all times, and he started criticizing her taste in just about everything, but particularly her taste in music.

If she were listening to a country music station, he would change it to jazz. "Show some class, Gessie," he would sneer at her.

The only time Gessie got to listen to her music was when she was jogging in the early morning. Burton worked out at the gym every morning and had insisted that Gessie work out also so she "wouldn't let her figure go."

Gessie hadn't argued with the concept, only the manner in which Burton had conveyed it. More like an order, not a suggestion. That had been happening more and more.

Gessie considered it a small victory when she had gone along with the exercise suggestion, but chose jogging instead of the gym, so that she would have some time to herself. Something else she was getting less and less of.

Then several things happened at almost the same time. Gessie was offered a management position with a sizable increase in pay. It should have been a good thing, but she hadn't been sure Burton would see it that way. He'd only be happy about it if he thought it somehow reflected well on him. But he could just as easily fly off the handle, because he generally didn't like to share the spotlight, even for a moment.

She needn't have worried. She hadn't gotten the chance to tell Burton about the offer. When she had gotten home that day, she had gone into the bedroom to change. She could hear Burton in the shower, and she had stood dumbfounded in the middle of the room. In the corner of the bedroom where her guitar case usually sat was a hideous-looking treadmill. If that weren't bad enough, she'd also noticed some white powder residue on a mirror lying atop Burton's chest of drawers.

When Burton came out of the shower, she'd confronted him about the cocaine, and he had dismissed her concerns entirely.

"Nothing wrong with getting a little boost now and then," Burton had smirked. "You should try it; maybe you'd loosen up a bit."

Gessie didn't bother to comment; in her mind, she was already walking out the door. That decision was solidified when she asked about the treadmill.

"I got it for you, Gessie. Now you won't have to go anywhere to jog. You can stay right here. It'll be much safer for you."

Gessie hadn't bought it for a minute. She didn't know what had taken her so long to see what a jerk he was. She had said as calmly as she could, "I know better, Burton. You're not concerned with my safety. This is just another way for you to make sure you know where I am and that I'm doing what you want me to do. What did you do with my guitar?"

Burton told her she was being ridiculous, but had finally told her he had put the guitar out in the garage. He had been right when he pointed out she hardly played it, but it was one of the few things in the house that was truly hers. It was the same guitar her parents had given her when she was ten, and it had always been a comfort to her just seeing it sitting in the corner.

As Gessie started toward the garage to find her guitar, Burton had begun shouting at her, telling her how ungrateful she was, how lucky she was that someone like him would be interested in her. At one point, Gessie thought

Burton was actually going to hit her. Instead, he walked out of the room, and said he was going to go blow off some steam.

"Don't wait up," Burton had snarled as he slammed the door leading into the garage.

Gessie had waited until he was gone. Then she'd gone out to the garage and found her guitar in a storage closet next to an old lawnmower. She opened the trunk of her car and placed the guitar inside. She walked back into the house and packed up anything she wanted to take with her. There really wasn't all that much. She'd always tried to keep her things to a minimum. She'd lived with Burton for several months, but nothing in the house was hers. She gathered her clothes from the closet, just leaving them on the hangars and laying them in the backseat of her car. She pulled clothes out of the dresser and packed them in her suitcase, stuffed all her toiletries into a backpack, and then grabbed her purse, cellphone, and laptop bag and carried it all out to the car.

She went back into the house and did a final walkthrough to make sure there was nothing else she wanted, then she went back to the garage, got in her car, and drove to the nearest hotel and got a room for the night. Once she was checked into her room, she opened her laptop and sent an email with her resignation to FMS. When she'd finally admitted she had made a colossal mistake with Burton, Gessie had also realized she didn't enjoy her job. She might have been really good at it, but it didn't make her happy, and a promotion to another position wouldn't have made a difference. Instead of accepting the promotion, she'd given FMS two weeks' notice, and since she was owed more than that in unused vacation time, it meant she would not be going back into the office. Ever.

She'd sent a second email to Burton telling him she had left for good and didn't care what he did with anything she might have forgotten to take with her. An email might have seemed cold to some people as a way to break up, but she remembered too well the look on Burton's face when she thought he had been going to punch her. She didn't want to give him a second chance.

Finally, she had picked up her cellphone and called her mother to let her know she was leaving California the next morning and would be home in a couple of days. Her mother had assumed it was just for a visit and was thrilled. Gessie hadn't seen any reason to go into the details of what had happened--that would be better face to face--and she'd wanted to be able to add what she had planned for the future. Something she hadn't completely figured out yet.

Around midnight, she had turned off her cellphone because Burton had begun texting and calling her every few minutes. She'd gotten up bright and early the next morning and set out from Palo Alto for Kansas City. As she cranked up the volume on her favorite country station, and belted out the songs as she drove, it became absolutely clear to her what she wanted to do.

CHAPTER 3

Gessie was saved from her trip down memory lane when she heard a knock at her door. It could really only be one person. Very few people found their way into the interior courtyard for the loft apartments off 2nd Avenue, and even fewer knew that Gessie lived in one of the lofts.

A quick check through the peephole, confirmed what Gessie already knew. Vanda Dalton was standing on her doorstep. Typical Vanda, she was sticking out her tongue and crossing her eyes, knowing Gessie was looking at her.

"Must you do that every time?" Gessie laughed as she opened the door.

"Just want you to know it's me."

"And you don't think the purple hair might tip me off?"

"You never know. I could change my hair color."

Gessie studied her friend for a moment. Besides the purple hair, she had an amethyst colored stud through her left eyebrow, and a sleeve of purple flowers tattooed down her right arm.

"I admit. It's hard to imagine you without the purple hair. Another color might fool me for a couple of minutes, but you do have a couple of other distinguishing characteristics."

"I could color my hair, take out the stud, and wear a long sleeve shirt."

"Okay, okay, you win."

"That was too easy. Something's eating at you. What is it?"

It had only been a month, but already the two women were like sisters. Gessie had met Vanda the first day she had moved into her apartment. Vanda lived directly across the courtyard from her, and the floor plans of their one-bedroom lofts were mirror images of each other. Vanda had shown up at Gessie's door that first day and introduced herself as the official Welcome Wagon for the loft complex. She had brought along a bottle of wine, a baguette and some cheese, and had proceeded to fill Gessie in on the other tenants in the complex while they shared the items Vanda had brought.

Gessie learned early on that anyone who took Vanda at face value was making a mistake. Vanda blamed her mother for her current look. She was named after a type of orchid her mother adored, and it had seemed the perfect name for her beautiful little girl. Growing up, most people had thought the name weird, and she suffered through years of questions and teasing because of it. She'd gone through a chubby stage where the kids called her Vanda Panda. In her awkward teenage years, she had been labeled Blanda Vanda, when she wasn't wearing whatever was the latest fad with the popular girls. Her senior year in high school, she had gotten the stud and colored her hair purple. That had shown the popular girls what she thought of them. Her freshman year of college, she had started on the tattoo sleeve of flowers. Of course, they were vandas.

Gessie would never get a tattoo and usually didn't like them on other people. But whoever had done the flowers down Vanda's arm was very good. The beautiful orchids were placed on her arm in such a way that made it easy to picture a garden full of the pretty flowers. Some were just budding, and others were in full bloom. The tattoo suited Vanda perfectly. And what Vanda had started as a means to be different and in-your-face rebellious had, instead, become a part of who she was. People usually couldn't keep their eyes off Vanda. The fact was she was beautiful, and those she let close found out she was also intelligent and fiercely loyal to her friends. Like Gessie, Vanda had graduated top in her class and had an MBA from Vanderbilt. She was a marketing genius and worked as a freelance consultant for many of the companies in the Nashville area.

Gessie smiled at her friend and invited her in.

"In answer to your question, I was thinking about Burton."

"I thought you'd put that jerk behind you. What made you go down that dark well?"

Gessie told Vanda about what had just happened on the street.

"So, let me get this straight. Some drunks were hassling you, and a gorgeous hunk of manhood came in to save the day, and not only didn't you stay around to thank him or give him your number or something, but you somehow twisted his chivalry into the possessive psychosis of good ol' Burton?"

"You have such a way with words, Vanda. I can take care of myself."

"Sure, you can. But it's nice to have someone else take some of the load now and then. Not every man is like Burton, Gessie. I know just the thing to get that creep off your mind. Let's go honky tonkin'. I was in the Harley store earlier, and I heard a couple of women talking about the Cole Trammel Band playing The Stage tonight."

"I don't think I've ever heard of them."

"I'm not surprised," countered Vanda. "They probably aren't well known unless you're from here. They started out doing the usual open mike nights and moved up from there. It wasn't long before they got noticed. The word is, they just got back in town after being on tour as an opening act for some big-name country star. I think you'll like them. And Cole Trammel is hot. The rest of the band aren't hard to look at either."

Vanda waggled her eyebrows and gave a little shimmy that made Gessie laugh.

"Okay, I'll go. But I've got to shower and change."

As Gessie showered, she tried to decide what to wear. At 5' 6", Gessie was the same height as Vanda. They even wore the same size, even if Vanda did fill out her clothes a little more than Gessie. Unlike a lot of friends, however, Gessie and Vanda wouldn't be borrowing each other's outfits anytime soon. Their styles were completely different. Vanda had obviously done a little shopping at the Harley store earlier. She had been wearing a new shirt Gessie hadn't seen before. It was a Harley Winged Cross Tee with a wide neckline that Vanda had let dip off one shoulder. Add in the pair of ripped skinny jeans, tucked into her turquoise-stitched boots, and Gessie knew it wouldn't matter what she decided to wear. All eyes would be on Vanda, and that was fine with Gessie. She wasn't looking for attention. She had come to Nashville for a reason, and it wasn't to find a man. She definitely wasn't looking for another relationship. Apparently, Burton wasn't as far forgotten as she would have wished. Maybe a night out was just what she needed.

She had learned two things very early on in Nashville. They never said Country Western, just Country, and a cowboy hat was optional. She decided not to wear hers. Instead, she pulled her long blond hair up into a messy knot on top of her head. She didn't want to take the time to style it, and it was still too hot out to wear it down. She put on a

Roper sleeveless white blouse, a pair of boot-cut jeans, and her favorite pair of ankle boots that were an antique white color with bronze stitching. She added a touch of mascara, blush, and lip gloss, and then went out into the living room where she found Vanda looking at a couple of sheets of music Gessie remembered leaving on the coffee table.

"This is good," said Vanda. "Do I get to hear it?"

"It's not ready," Gessie said as she hurried across the room and held out her hand.

Vanda gave a little shrug and handed the sheets of paper to Gessie. "Really good, Gessie."

"It's not ready," Gessie insisted. "But I promise. You'll be the first to hear it."

Gessie didn't want to show how excited she was to hear Vanda liked the song she had written. Vanda's opinion was important to Gessie, and Vanda really did know music. Just one more of Vanda's many talents. She was an accomplished pianist, and even people who knew her well were surprised to learn she preferred classical music. That didn't mean she didn't know and appreciate other music, however, and she had been Gessie's biggest fan right from the start. Gessie thought the new song was good, but she really did have a few things she still wanted to tweak.

Vanda was giving her that "You'd better not be lying to me" look.

"I promise. Soon. You'll hear it. For now, let's go honky tonkin'."

The two women made a striking pair as they walked out onto 2nd Avenue and made their way toward the neon lights of lower Broadway. Vanda looked like she'd be right at home revving up the motor of a Harley low-rider, while Gessie would be more apt to take the reins of a mustang. A Shelby Mustang that is. She liked to feel the wind as she drove, too. But a convertible was more her speed. Their styles might have been different, but there was no doubt they were both in the mood for some fun.

It was a weeknight, and the summer tourist season was over. Although there was a good crowd at The Stage, there was at least room to move around, and even a few open seats at the bar.

Heads turned as Gessie and Vanda walked through the crowd and chose a couple of stools at the bar. They had a good view of the stage where a young woman was playing an acoustic guitar, and doing a cover of a recent Miranda Lambert hit. The Stage actually had several different levels, and different music acts scheduled for each. The young girl on the stage now was pretty good, but Gessie didn't think she was good enough to be a featured act. At least not yet. As usual, Vanda didn't waste any time finding out if the information she had gotten at the Harley store was correct.

"Is Cole Trammel playing the main stage tonight?" Vanda asked the bartender when he came over to get their drink orders.

"Their set starts in just a few minutes," the man nodded. "What can I get you?"

Gessie and Vanda each ordered a beer and listened to the last strains of the young girl's song.

"She's not bad. You're better," Vanda said. "This would be a good place for you to break in."

Gessie didn't say anything. Vanda had been encouraging her from the start. But Gessie wasn't ready yet. She had been away from her music for quite some time. So, she was content to work on her original material and was developing her own style in the process. For now, busking was fine for her. She wasn't in any hurry. When she was ready, she might sign up for one of the open mike nights in the area and see how it went from there.

"You're in for a real treat, folks," a man announced after stepping up to the mike on the stage. "The Cole Trammel Band is back after being part of the Nashville Hot Tour, and they're here on the main stage tonight. Let's hear it for Cole Trammel!"

Gessie watched as four men walked onto the stage. As the spotlight caught the slender man who stepped up to the microphone, Gessie gave a little gasp.

"What?" Vanda asked.

"That's him. That's the guy who chased off the drunks who were hassling me earlier."

"And you let him just walk off? There's something wrong with you, woman." Vanda could have saved her breath.

Gessie hadn't heard her. Her eyes were riveted on Cole Trammel.

Cole was saying something about being happy to be back home and seeing old friends. His gaze was sweeping the room as he talked, and when he looked over toward the bar, his eyes landed on Gessie. "And I'm hoping to meet some new friends, too, and hear all the music I've missed while I was gone."

His eyes had lingered on Gessie for a moment more, and then he had turned to his bandmates to signal the start of their first song. Gessie found herself truly enjoying the band's music. They did a few cover songs, but for the most part, the songs were original and had a unique blend of old and new country.

Several times during the set, Vanda had nudged Gessie. "He's looking right at you."

"Don't be silly," Gessie had protested. But she knew better. She hadn't taken her eyes off Cole Trammel for a minute, and he had definitely looked directly at her. Every time, Gessie felt like a volt of electricity had run through her. She'd never had that type of reaction to a guy, and it scared her a little bit.

The band had been playing for about an hour when Cole stepped up to the mike and announced they would be taking a fifteen-minute break. He handed his guitar to the bass player beside him and then jumped off the stage, headed toward the bar.

"We should probably go," Gessie said as she stood up from her barstool.

Vanda didn't move. "Oh no, you don't. Here he comes."

Before she knew it, Cole Trammel was standing in front of her.

"I'm glad you came to see me. I feel better knowing you're okay."

Gessie bristled somewhat. "I didn't come to see you. I mean, I didn't know it was you I was coming to see, and of course I'm okay. I can take care of myself."

Vanda was staring at Gessie with an open mouth. She turned to Cole Trammel and held out her hand. "Hi, I'm Vanda Dalton. What my friend here meant was, she wanted to thank you for stepping in when those drunks were hassling her. Isn't that right, Gessie?"

Cole chuckled and shook Vanda's extended hand. "Nice to meet you, Vanda. I seem to have offended your friend. Gessie, is it?"

"Gessie Chapel," Vanda responded, clearly enjoying herself.

Gessie had been scowling at the exchange between Vanda and Cole, and she was caught off guard when Cole suddenly turned to her. "I'm sure you can take care of yourself, but my mama taught me better than to stand idly by if I sensed something was going on that wasn't right."

Cole then extended his hand toward Gessie. "Truce?"

There wasn't anything Gessie could do but shake his hand. It would have been rude not to, and her mama had taught her a few manners, too. She wasn't sure why she had overreacted earlier or why she had done so again just now. "Truce," agreed Gessie as she took his offered hand.

If she'd thought making eye contact with Cole had given her a jolt, it was nothing compared to when he took her hand. She wouldn't have been surprised if sparks had flown. Her breath caught, and she was barely able to get out her next words, "Th-thank you. For earlier."

The handshake should have ended at that point, but neither Gessie nor Cole had let go. Cole's eyes had met hers, and his gaze was so intense Gessie felt weak in the knees. She had to get a hold of herself.

Vanda knew Gessie well and knew she was about to lock up. She needed some space. Vanda could see things were happening too fast for her friend. So, she took charge of the moment.

"Oh, I'm sorry, but we really need to go. It was nice meeting you, Cole. We really love your music. Looks like your band is ready to start back up. Come on, Gessie." Vanda had tugged on Gessie's free hand and gently pulled her away from Cole as she was talking, and she was already steering Gessie toward the door.

It wasn't until Gessie had left the bar that Cole turned and hopped back on the stage to start the next set with his band.

CHAPTER 4

As soon as they hit the sidewalk in front of The Stage, Gessie turned to Vanda. "You want to tell me what just happened in there?"

"What just happened in there was I saved you from yourself. Anybody could see the connection between the two of you. It looked to me like it was physical, too, and it scared the bejeebers out of you. Who knows what you would have done? Something stupid. That's for sure."

"I wasn't scared."

"You're still scared. You got gobsmacked, and you don't want to admit it. I told you Cole Trammel was hot."

"And I'm not about to get burned."

"No reason you have to. But that doesn't mean you shouldn't get to know him. He's obviously smitten with you."

"Bejeebers, gobsmacked, smitten? You're even talking crazy, Vanda. Besides, I'll probably never see him again."

"Don't be so sure about that. Nashville can be a small town when it wants to be, especially within the music community. I'm guessing it won't be too hard for him to find you, and I have no doubt it'll be soon. Want to make a bet on it?"

Gessie didn't want to bet on it. She didn't even want to think about it. Unfortunately, Vanda wasn't helping with that.

"I've got a meeting with a client down in Franklin tomorrow. So, I won't be around until later. How about we plan to go somewhere for dinner together, and you can tell me all about you and Cole Trammel. Unless you are going to dinner with him, of course."

Gessie continued to protest that Cole Trammel wasn't interested in her any more than she was interested in him. But it fell on deaf ears. Vanda just gave her a smug grin as she walked toward the door to her condo.

"Save it. And I want all the details at dinner tomorrow evening. I'd wish you sweet dreams, but I think "sweet" might not be the right word for dreams of Cole Trammel."

As Gessie unlocked the door to her condo, Vanda's parting words stayed with her. She had no doubt she was going to be having trouble sleeping, and there was even less of a doubt that it would be because of Cole Trammel. She really couldn't get him out of her head. And although it made no sense, it was like she could still feel him holding her hand, and just the thought of that had her heart racing.

She needed to calm herself, and the best way she knew to do that was to pick up her guitar. She walked over to her guitar case and popped the latches. She couldn't help the smile that spread across her face when she opened the lid. Seeing her guitar always made her smile. It was like an old friend.

Although it had been new to her when she received it on her tenth birthday, her father had found the used instrument in a local pawn shop. It was an Epiphone Troubadour model made in the 70s. It had a good tone and a tapered neck that had made it easier for the small hands of a ten-year-old to play. It wasn't an expensive guitar, and some would say it wasn't of very high quality. It certainly didn't compare to the original Epiphones, or those made by its parent company, Gibson. Regardless. Gessie loved it.

She picked the guitar up gently from the case and took it over with her to the sofa. She knew she was too keyed up to work on the song she had been writing. So, she just absently began plucking the strings. Her eyes practically flew open when she realized she was playing the lead in to "Bless the Broken Road" by Rascal Flats. True, it was one of her favorite songs. But the fact that it had popped into her head, and had been communicated so easily to her fingers, was more than a bit unsettling. Was the song right? Had everything led her here? To Nashville. To Cole.

29

* * *

Not surprisingly, Gessie hadn't slept well. She had tossed and turned. Her dreams were a jumbled mix of Burton and Cole, and both men made her uneasy, but for entirely different reasons. Gessie was actually relieved when she looked at the clock and saw it was 5:30 a.m. One of the good things that had come of her bad relationship with Burton was her morning runs.

Jogging had originally been a necessity. It had been the only way to get away from Burton and be alone for a short period of time. Now, jogging was a joy. She still liked the time to herself, and she'd found the peace and solitude freed her mind to think about her music. There were many days after a run when she'd sit right down with whatever song she was working on at the time, and the phrase or the notes she had been looking for, flowed smoothly from her mind to the paper. She wasn't sure she could keep her mind free enough to think about music this morning. She'd be happy if she could just clear her mind of Cole Trammel.

Gessie unlocked the gate that opened from the courtyard onto 1st Avenue just as the first hint of dawn began to lighten the sky. She made sure her phone, her apartment and gate keys, and her canister of mace were secure in the fanny pack she always wore when she jogged. She then crossed the street and turned to her right. She varied her route, but today she had decided she was starting early enough that she could run down to the Nashville Train Station on Broadway. The first commuter train wouldn't arrive for another half hour, and she'd be there and on her way back before the area got busy with the first group of people arriving to start their day's work in downtown Nashville. She'd turn around at that point and run back along the Riverfront, past Fort Nashborough, and up through Bicentennial and Public Square Park before turning back again toward home.

At first, Gessie thought her mind was playing tricks on her. She had just reached the small plaza before the train station, when she saw a man pacing in front of one of the benches that lined the plaza. From the way he was dressed, he could have been any other jogger out at this time of the morning to beat the heat that was predicted for later in the day. But there was something familiar about him. She could have sworn it was Cole. She'd only gotten a glimpse of the man's face before he had turned to pace in the opposite direction. He had a phone to his ear and was obviously agitated as he spoke to whoever was on the other end of the call.

The man turned, and Gessie saw she had been right. It was Cole Trammel. Now that he was off the phone, his shoulders slumped, and he focused his attention on the park bench where a man lay curled in a fetal position. Gessie sensed something was wrong, and she picked up her pace.

31

She was still a few yards away when Cole looked up and noticed her.

"Gessie?" he asked. At first confused, Cole's tone changed to one of urgency. "Don't come any closer, Gessie."

Gessie stopped in her tracks, and it was then she heard sirens in the distance.

"Cole, is everything okay?"

"No, it's not, Gessie. The police are on their way. Get out of here so that you don't get caught up in this."

Gessie didn't know what he thought she would get caught up in, but it didn't really matter. She hated anyone telling her what to do, particularly some man who thought he knew what was best for her. Gessie chided herself. Cole wasn't Burton, and while it was true she didn't like being told what to do, the real reason she wasn't going to leave was because she could tell how shaken Cole was with whatever was happening. She had a feeling he might need a friendly face at some point.

Cole took one look at Gessie's face and seemed to understand she had no intention of leaving. He might have been going to say something, but he didn't get the chance because a police car had screeched to a stop at the curb, followed closely by an ambulance.

Gessie walked back to the end of the plaza and took a seat on the farthest bench. She watched as two EMTs jumped out of the ambulance and ran toward the bench where Cole was pointing. A police officer got out of the patrol car and followed close behind the EMTs.

Whatever had happened to the man on the bench must have been evident to the EMTs, and it must have also been obvious there was nothing they could do for the man. The police officer spoke into a device of some sort on his shoulder and then took out a notebook and walked to where Cole was standing. It was clear he was questioning Cole, and at one point, he must have asked Cole something that made the officer turn and look over at where Gessie was sitting.

As the officer began walking toward her, she could see the scowl on Cole's face. He continued to watch as the officer reached her.

"Ma'am?" the officer started, "did you see what happened here?"

"Not really, officer. I was jogging and thought I recognized Cole over there. When I got closer to him, I also noticed there was someone on the bench, and Cole told me I should stay back. And that's when you arrived. So, I just moved over here to wait."

"What was Mr. Trammel doing when you first noticed him?"

"He was pacing a short distance from the bench and talking to someone on the phone."

"And how do you know Mr. Trammel?"

"I just met him last night. His band was performing at The Stage."

"What about the man on the bench? Do you know him?"

"I have no idea whether I know him or not. I didn't get close enough. It's doubtful, though. I've only been in Nashville for about a month, and I haven't met many people."

The officer took down her name and contact information and then told her she would need to stay and speak with the detective who would be on the scene soon. Cole had moved a distance away from the bench and had resumed pacing. He had looked over at Gessie several times but had obviously been told he had to stay where he was.

Gessie watched as additional people arrived on the scene. Like anyone who had seen a TV drama, Gessie could guess who the new arrivals were and what they were doing. Two more patrol cars had come up, and the officers were positioned to make sure the scene stayed secure since the first commuter train would be arriving any minute, disgorging people at the nearby station. The medical examiner and an assistant arrived along with a man who Gessie figured was a detective. After several minutes of activity, the detective left the medical examiner and his assistant with the body, and he walked over to Cole.

Cole became quite animated as he talked to the detective. At one point, Cole raised his voice, and it sounded like he shouted, "No. Somebody did this!" They seemed to argue some more, and then the detective turned away from Cole and made a phone call. Once he'd hung up, he began walking over toward Gessie.

The detective was what Gessie always thought of as ruggedly handsome. He looked to be slightly taller than Cole and more solidly built. He was wearing a sport coat over a light blue Oxford shirt and a pair of jeans. He had short, sandy brown hair, and as he got closer, Gessie could see he had piercingly blue eyes. Those eyes were looking at her very intently.

Gessie could feel him assessing her as she stood up. She found herself wishing she was wearing something other than her running clothes.

"Miss Chapel?" the detective asked after consulting a small notebook he held in his hand.

"Gessie."

"Okay, Gessie. I'm Detective Warner with the Metropolitan Nashville PD Investigations Unit. Can you tell me what you saw happen here?"

Gessie repeated for the detective what she had told the officer. He asked a few more questions about her relationship with Cole. But when he seemed satisfied she really had just met him, he moved on.

"And you didn't get a look at the dead man?"

"No, I didn't get close to him. I guess I just assumed he was a homeless man who had slept on the bench. I see them some mornings when I'm out jogging."

"Does the name Gary Armbruster mean anything to you?"

"No. I'm sorry," Gessie answered, shaking her head. "Like I said, I'm pretty new in town. Is that who the man was?"

The detective didn't answer her question. He gave her a final look and then handed her a business card with the instruction to call him if she remembered anything else about the incident.

She was oddly unsettled by the detective. She had a feeling he could be very intimidating if he chose to be. He hadn't been that way with her, however. He had been serious, professional, but she could sense an underlying compassion. She found him very interesting. He wasn't like anyone she had ever encountered before.

She watched as Detective Warner walked to where the medical examiner and his assistant were in the process of zipping the dead man into a body bag and lifting him onto a gurney. Cole walked beside the gurney as it was wheeled across the plaza to a van parked at the curb. Once the doors were closed, Cole turned back and walked to where Detective Warner was now talking with one of the officers maintaining the perimeter.

Gessie thought Cole looked angry as he walked toward the two men. When Detective Warner saw Cole approaching, he seemed to anticipate what was on Cole's mind and pointed behind Cole to another van that had pulled up to the curb. Cole turned around and watched as a man and a woman got out of the van. The woman started walking toward Detective Warner while the man went to the back of the van and grabbed a case of some kind.

Cole had stopped and seemed a lot less angry with the arrival of what Gessie assumed were crime scene technicians. Detective Warner talked with the female technician for a couple of minutes, and then he walked to where Cole was standing and gave him a card just as he had done with Gessie.

CHAPTER 5

The circumstances might have been less than optimum, but that didn't mean Gessie couldn't appreciate Cole's long, lean body as he walked toward her. He was wearing running shorts and a t-shirt, both of which showed off a physique with not a hint of body fat. He wasn't some muscled gym rat. He was just well-toned and, well, perfect in Gessie's eyes.

She gave him a half-smile when he had reached where she was waiting. "Are you okay, Cole?"

"Gessie, what are you doing here? Why did you stay?"

"You looked pretty upset. I just thought you might want a friendly face when whatever happened was over."

Cole seemed to really look at her then. He studied her face and then took in the rest of her. She felt herself blushing as she caught something flash briefly in his eyes. For the second time that morning, she realized she had quite a bit of herself on display. With only a sports bra and a pair of running shorts, there wasn't much left to the imagination.

Well, there was nothing she could do about it at the moment, and the look in Cole's eyes passed, to be replaced with one of sadness.

"Hey, I just live down the street. Do you want to talk about what happened? I could make some coffee, and I'm a good listener."

That brought a hint of a smile to Cole's face. "I'd like that."

Gessie looked back toward the train station and saw Detective Warner had been watching the exchange between her and Cole. She had the feeling he was still watching them as they walked down 1st Avenue.

When they reached Fort Nashborough, Gessie pointed across the street. "We can cross here and enter through the courtyard."

They each swiveled to check both ways for any traffic. It was quite a distance away, but as Gessie looked down the street back toward the train station, she saw she had been right. A solitary figure stood at the edge of the plaza. She was sure it was Detective Warner. She didn't have time to think about why the detective was still watching them, however, because she heard Cole saying it was clear for them to cross.

They darted across the street, and Gessie reached into her fanny pack and pulled out the key to the gate.

"This is nice," Cole said as they walked through the courtyard. "How long have you lived here?"

"Only a month," Gessie answered as she stopped in front of her door.

She didn't get a chance to add anything else because Vanda chose that moment to walk out of her apartment. Vanda took one look at Gessie and Cole and raised an eyebrow.

"Good morning, Gessie. Nice to see you again, Cole."

Gessie knew she'd be in for an "I told you so" conversation later. But she needed to hurry her friend along. Cole had nodded a good morning, but Gessie knew he wasn't up for the whirlwind that was Vanda. So, she put on a bright and cheery voice as she said hello to Vanda, hoping her friend would pick up on the fact she didn't want any further conversation right then.

"Good morning, Vanda. Be sure and drive carefully. I'll see you later."

Vanda did pick up on it. Gessie could tell by the slight scowl and the way Vanda had said she'd be looking forward to it as she walked out of the courtyard.

Once inside her apartment, Gessie told Cole she would start the coffee, and then was just going to pop upstairs to splash some water on her face. She pointed Cole to the small washroom just off the entryway if he wanted to do the same. After setting up the coffee machine, Gessie raced up the stairs to the bedroom loft. She freshened up a bit and did a quick change into a pair of jean shorts and a t-shirt.

When she got back downstairs, Cole was sitting at the dining table with his head in his hands. Gessie didn't say anything. She went into the kitchen and poured them each a mug of coffee. Cole looked up as she set one of the mugs in front of him.

"Do you need cream or sugar?" Gessie asked.

"No, just black. Thanks, Gessie. This is nice of you. I like your apartment."

Gessie sensed Cole wasn't ready yet to talk about what happened. So, she told him about finding the apartment.

"I was fortunate they had an opening here. I wasn't ready to buy a place right away. I wanted to get to know the area. This apartment was perfect for me. It's inspiring to be here downtown and to experience all the music. I loved your band, by the way."

At the mention of his band, Cole's eyes wandered over to the corner of the room where her guitar case was propped up. "I didn't get to hear you out on the street yesterday. What kind of music do you play?"

"Country, of course," Gessie grinned.

That got a slight smile from Cole, and he took a sip of his coffee.

"Do you want to talk about what happened?" Gessie asked gently. "Was the man on the bench a friend of yours?"

Cole nodded but didn't say anything right away. Gessie took another sip of her coffee and waited.

"His name is...was...Gary Armbruster and he and I grew up together. In high school, Buddy Norman, Spence Appleby, Gary, and I formed a band."

Gessie couldn't help herself. She gasped. "That was one of the guys in your band?"

Cole looked surprised and confused at the same time.

"What? No. Sorry. Gary isn't in the band anymore."

Gessie felt really bad for interrupting, especially because Cole looked so sad when he said Gary wasn't in the band anymore.

"Hey, I'm sorry I interrupted. I said I'd listen. I'll be quiet. I promise. That is if you still want to talk about it."

"Yeah, actually. But to talk about what happened today, I need to go back a way. We all grew up around music," Cole began, "and I guess you could say we were all naturals. We played all kinds of music back then. Mostly whatever anyone wanted to hear. We played at school dances, fairs, churches, and a wedding reception or two, doing mostly covers of other artists' songs. Gary could play anything with strings, and he had a great voice and a real knack for harmony. Buddy's real name is Dylan, but he got the nickname Buddy when he started beating on anything in sight at the age of two. His dad would joke Dylan was the next Buddy Rich and the nickname stuck. I played the guitar and some fiddle and was the lead singer. Spence played the bass guitar, and did some vocals and harmony, too."

Gessie sipped her coffee and listened in silence as Cole went on to explain that by the time they graduated from high school, the band was starting to have a few problems. Buddy had always preferred rock over country and kept trying to steer the band in that direction. Buddy's dad owned a string of car dealerships throughout Tennessee, and the family was very well off. His dad had given Buddy a full-size SUV for his sixteenth birthday, and that was what they used to haul themselves and their equipment to wherever they were playing. Buddy thought that made him the leader of their band, and he had started balking whenever they accepted a country gig. Both Spence and Cole preferred country, and much to Buddy's displeasure, they even preferred the old-style country. Not the rock country or rap country that was starting to pop up all over Nashville. Gary didn't care one way or the other. He just liked to play and didn't like confrontations.

"Then, our senior year of high school," Cole said, "the real problems started. Her name was Rhonda Baxter. She could sing, really sing. She was kind of a combo of the Wilson sisters. Rhonda could sing country, but it was with songs like Heart's "Crazy on You" that she really got into it. Naturally, she tried to influence the band in that direction. Everybody had a crush on Rhonda, but Gary was head over heels, and Rhonda played on that.

"Gary had been my closest friend, but his relationship with Rhonda trumped that. Gary started to side with Buddy and Rhonda, and every decision for the band came up three against two. Ultimately that meant we became a rock band. Spence and I went along, but we weren't really enjoying it much anymore, and there was definitely tension. By the time we graduated, the band had broken up. It might have happened anyway, because we were all going our separate ways. Spence got a football scholarship to the University of Tennessee, and I had decided I wanted to go for a degree in Music at Belmont University. Buddy didn't see any reason to go to college since he knew he was going to work for his dad, and he got Gary a job, too. Rhonda..."

Cole started to continue but was interrupted when his cellphone rang. He popped the phone out of the holder he had attached to an armband he wore on his left arm. Gessie listened to his side of the brief conversation, but since it consisted mostly of one word, yes or no answers, she didn't get much out of it.

"That was Detective Warner with the MNPD," Cole told Gessie as he ended the call. "I'm sorry. I've got to go. I've got to go down to the station. The good news is I convinced the detective that Gary wouldn't have OD'd, especially not that way. The bad news is they're now looking at it as a suspicious death, and it sounds like I'm their prime suspect."

"He said he thought you murdered Gary?" gasped Gessie.

"No. He was much more subtle. He says he just wanted some more information. I've got to call my lawyer and go home and change."

"Lawyer?"

They had both stood up from the table, and Cole stepped toward Gessie and gave her a quick kiss on the cheek. "Gessie, I can't tell you how grateful I am that you were there for me earlier and that you sat here and listened to me. There's a lot more to the story, though. Can I call you?"

Everything had ended so abruptly. Gessie still didn't know what had happened with Gary. Cole was standing only inches away from her. It had just been a peck on the cheek, but Gessie could still feel the warmth spreading through her. It was all she could do not to touch her hand to her cheek in wonder. It took a moment for her to find her voice.

"Yes, please call me. If there's anything I can do to help, let me know. Can I give you a ride or something?"

Cole had stepped back a bit, tapped the Contacts app on his phone, and handed it to Gessie so she could enter in her information.

"I only live a few blocks from here. I like to walk. Thanks again, Gessie," Cole added as he took back his phone and strapped it into his armband.

Gessie walked him to the door and pointed out the exit from the courtyard onto 2nd Avenue. Before she knew it, he was gone from sight, and she was feeling somewhat dazed as she closed the door and went back inside her apartment. She was definitely at loose ends and not quite sure what she wanted to do. It was still too early to go on the street and do any busking. She wasn't sure she was in the mood to do that anyway. And if she wasn't in the mood to do that, she knew for sure she wouldn't have the focus to make any progress with the song she had been working on.

She picked up the coffee mugs off the table and took them into the kitchen. Another cup of coffee was out of the question. She was too wired. She decided she should eat something. Maybe that would help calm herself down. She went for her "go-to" comfort food—peanut butter toast. Gessie put a couple of slices of bread in the toaster and reached into the cabinet for a jar of creamy peanut butter. The minute the bread popped up out of the toaster, Gessie began spreading a thin layer of peanut butter on each slice. Her mouth was already watering as she watched the peanut butter melting on the hot slices of bread. She took a quick bite of toast, and then grabbed a bottle of orange juice from the fridge and set it, along with the toast, on the countertop that was the separation between the kitchen and the living/dining area of the apartment. It was where Gessie ate most of her meals. She only used the table when she had company. Until this morning, that had only been when Vanda had joined her, usually to share takeout one or the other of them had ordered. Cole was the only person besides Vanda who had ever been in her apartment.

Thinking of Cole, Gessie took another bite of the peanut butter toast, but before sitting down, she made a quick detour to the end table in the living room where she had left her laptop charging. She took the laptop with her over to the countertop and flipped open the lid. As she waited for the laptop to boot up, she took a sip of her juice, and worked on finishing off the first slice of toast. As she chewed, her mind had been mapping out what she wanted to research on her laptop.

Cole really hadn't told her much before he'd had to leave. He had said Gary had OD'd and that he didn't think Gary would have done that himself. That meant Cole thought Gary had been murdered. She really had no idea just how Gary had OD'd, and if Cole had any idea who might have done such a thing, he hadn't gotten to that point in his story. Maybe he wouldn't have shared his suspicions anyway.

Gessie couldn't explain even to herself how she could feel so close to Cole after seeing him for the first time only the day before. That's just the way it was, and she had no desire to do anything other than try to help him. Gary's death had upset him, and her only thought was to try to help Cole find out what had happened. To do that, Gessie would need more information. She could wait until Cole called her and told her the rest of his story. She had no doubt that he would. The question was whether or not she should just sit and wait until he did, or if she should find out whatever she could on her own. She wouldn't even have to mention whatever she learned unless it would help Cole in some way.

Having justified what she was about to do in her own mind, Gessie finished the last bite of peanut butter toast and began her first search.

CHAPTER 6

What not too many people, and certainly no one in Nashville, knew was that Gessie was a computer whiz. In her early years, she had developed some fairly impressive hacking skills. It was probably a good thing for everyone that Gessie didn't exercise those skills. Well, that wasn't exactly true. She might have exercised them. She just didn't usually follow through. She had no problem hacking into her high school's database, for instance, but she had never changed a record. She wouldn't have done it for anybody else, and in her case, there was no need to. She already had top grades in all her classes.

When she had developed the program for Financial Management Systems, she had programmed in a back door. Only she knew about it, and she was confident she was the only one who'd ever be able to access it. It wasn't that she ever would, but there was a part of her that liked knowing it was there.

Since she had left California, her job, and Burton behind, she hadn't used her computer for anything other than online shopping, email, and a music app she sometimes played with. That didn't mean she had forgotten anything. For her, it was like remembering how to ride a bicycle. Her fingers fairly flew across the keyboard. With social media, it was doubtful she would even need to do any hacking. It was amazing how much information you could find out through a simple Google search.

She decided the best place to start was to learn more about the Cole Trammel Band. She wasn't surprised when the first link that showed up was to the band's website. What did surprise her were several links to articles about a lawsuit. "Local Band Sued for Stealing Lyrics to Hit Song" seemed to sum up the theme of the articles from various Nashville newspapers.

Gessie was tempted to dive immediately into the links about the lawsuit, but decided to hold off. She clicked on the link for the band's website, and her screen was immediately filled with a picture of the band posed in front of a tired-looking pickup truck. Cole was the central figure, with one foot positioned on the running board by the driver's side door, and a melancholy smile on his handsome face. One of the band members was looking out from under the raised hood, one was on the far side of the truck bed with his arms crossed atop the rail, and the fourth member was sitting on the open tailgate.

Whoever had choreographed the picture had done an
excellent job. While your eyes were initially drawn to Cole,
you couldn't help but look at each of the other band
members as well. The picture gave you the impression that
something was up, and if you studied each of the band
members, you might figure out what it was. Gessie smiled
and then clicked on the "About the Band" link, where she
found bios on each of the men.

Gessie congratulated herself when she read the bios
about Spence Appleby and Trey Hargrove. When the band
had interrupted the two drunks who had hassled her, her
impression had been of Cole as a Quarterback, and the guys
with him as his linemen. She'd been right on the mark with
Spence and Trey. While the information highlighted their
musical background, it also mentioned that both Spence
and Trey had played football at the University of Tennessee.
Spence played bass in the band, and Cole had said the two
of them had gone to High School together. Since he hadn't
mentioned Trey Hargrove, Gessie assumed it was Trey's
connection with Spence that led to his inclusion in the band
as their drummer.

The last member of the band was Matt Harrison, the lead
guitarist. He wasn't quite as big as the other two men, and
there was no mention that he had played football. It did say
he had gone to Belmont University, and had a passion for
teaching as well as playing music. He had met Cole while at
Belmont, and Cole had enticed him into joining the band.

There was no mention of Gary Armbruster having been in the band initially. There was also no mention of Buddy Norman or Rhonda Baxter, not that Gessie expected there to be. It was only Gary who Cole had said was originally in what was his current band. She made a note to herself to Google Rhonda and both men later.

Before she left the website, Gessie clicked on the Music link, which had a picture of the same pickup truck that had been on the main page. This time, only Cole was in the picture, with "Tired of Leaving" and "Cole Trammel" stamped on the song cover. This was obviously the hit single mentioned in the links she had seen about a lawsuit. The rest of the page was filled with pictures from the recent tour.

Gessie bookmarked the site. She wanted to come back and look at the site again later, and she definitely wanted to listen to the song clip. She had heard it the night before when she had been at The Stage. But she wanted to listen to it again now that she knew it was the subject of a lawsuit. She couldn't help but wonder if it had some connection to Gary Armbruster's murder. If so, she could understand why Cole would want an attorney with him when he went to the Nashville Police Station to talk with Detective Warner.

There were several sites with information about the lawsuit, and Gessie needed to look through all of them to get a handle on what had happened. Like most things online, there was conflicting information. The suit had not yet gone to trial. So, there wasn't much detail. The gist, however, seemed to be that Gary Armbruster had filed the suit, claiming he had co-written both the music and lyrics for "Tired of Leaving." Although neither Gary nor Cole had provided any comment for the articles, other than to refer the reporters to their attorneys, Buddy Norman seemed to be quoted frequently. Buddy was referred to as "prominent local businessman, Buddy Norman." Buddy had talked up his school days with both Gary and Cole and had stated that Cole had always taken advantage of Gary, who was painted as a trusting and faithful friend. Buddy said it was obvious Cole had kicked Gary out of his band because he wanted to record the song the two of them had written together, but Cole didn't want to share the limelight.

Buddy Norman certainly painted Cole in an awful light. It made her wonder what Buddy had against Cole. Somehow, she just couldn't see Cole doing what Buddy had said in the newspaper articles. And Cole had been devastated by Gary's death. It wasn't the reaction you expect out of the callous man Buddy Norman portrayed Cole to be.

Gessie wanted to know more about Buddy Norman. When she searched on his name, she got page upon page of hits. A good number of them seemed to be YouTube links featuring commercials for his car dealership. She selected one of the links at random and watched a video that featured a sexy young woman welcoming everyone to the Buddy Norman Autoplex as she walked along a row of cars, pointing out the current specials. She finished up her spiel by encouraging everyone to "Come on down today, and Buddy Norman will drum up a deal for you!" The camera panned to a man seated behind a set of drums. This was obviously Buddy Norman, and he was madly playing a drum solo as the dealership's slogan scrolled across the screen. He executed his final drum roll and then stood as he brought his drumsticks down for a loud clash of the cymbals. The video ended with a triumphant looking Buddy Norman standing with drumsticks in hand under the Buddy Norman Autoplex sign.

There were several different versions of the commercial using the same slogan and featuring a drum solo by Buddy Norman. Drum soloes were never Gessie's thing, but she had to admit he sounded pretty good, even if the commercial itself was a little hokey.

Local car dealership commercials had been done tongue in cheek since the days of the Cal Worthington commercials out in California. Cal used to have a musical jingle and featured his dog, Spot. The visual joke was that the dog was actually a full-grown tiger. It seemed like most local companies realized their commercials were not going to come off with the same quality as those done by a Fortune 500 company that had help from the best PR and Marketing firms. So, they went with the sincere, homespun, comical, or outlandish.

Gessie thought the Buddy Norman Autoplex commercials fell somewhere in between the comical and the outlandish, hence the hokey vibe. She had a feeling Buddy Norman wouldn't like to hear her opinion. He gave Gessie the impression he was totally serious about the drum solo. He was good looking, and might even have been handsome, if weren't for the arrogance that came out so clearly in the closeups of his face.

From the other articles Gessie found on the internet, Buddy was somewhat active in the business community, and there were pictures of him attending various charity events. His dark hair was slicked back, and he looked to have a perpetual tan. Buddy usually had a beautiful woman on his arm and was smiling broadly at the camera. However, the smile didn't seem to go all the way to his eyes, and Gessie got the feeling he was bored or impatient in most of the photos. She noticed the woman in the commercial was on Buddy's arm in a couple of the earlier articles, and she played a hunch.

She typed "Rhonda Baxter" into the search window and found a link to a couple of articles and her Facebook page. The sexy girl in the Buddy Norman commercials was Rhonda Baxter. Cole hadn't gotten the chance to tell her what happened to Rhonda, but from the entries on her Facebook page, it looked like she had tried to cash in on the Buddy Norman commercials. However, there were links to only a couple of other local ads. It didn't look like Rhonda had been all that successful. She now listed her occupation as a sales associate at none other than the Buddy Norman

Autoplex. She'd have to remember to ask Cole whatever happened to the relationship between Gary and Rhonda.

As Gessie shut down her laptop and sat back in her chair, she had to smile to herself. She had immediately decided she didn't like Buddy Norman or Rhonda Baxter. While she trusted her instincts, she had to admit her initial reaction had probably been influenced by the fact Buddy had spoken out against Cole, and Rhonda had gotten in between him and Gary. After reading that first article about the lawsuit, she had been predispositioned to find fault with the commercials as well as the pictures of Buddy and Rhonda at the various events around town. Of course, she had sensed Cole didn't much care for Buddy or Rhonda either. That definitely would have influenced her opinion as well.

She wanted to help find out what had happened to Gary, and she wondered if Buddy or Rhonda might know something. It sounded like Buddy had been around Gary a lot more than Cole had in recent years. She wasn't sure Gary and Rhonda were still dating each other. But she could still know a lot about him. It was possible either Buddy or Rhonda would know where Gary got his drugs, or if he'd made any enemies. People did crazy things to feed their drug habit. Gessie thought Detective Warner should be concentrating on that aspect of Gary's life instead of wasting time trying to tie Cole to the murder.

She looked at the clock on her wall, and although she had spent a couple of hours researching, she thought it was still too soon for her to call or text Cole. For all she knew, he could still be sitting at the police station answering questions. He had given her the feeling he would be calling her later. So, she just needed to be patient. Not an easy thing for her to do.

She'd already decided she wasn't going to go out busking and needed something else to keep herself busy. She straightened up the apartment a little and then made up a list of things she needed to pick up at the store. The Urban Market was only a few blocks away on Church Street. If she kept her list to a minimum, she would be able to fit everything into the large backpack she had bought for just that purpose. And she'd get the exercise she had missed out on earlier that morning when her run had been cut short.

After switching out her shorts for a pair of ankle jeans, Gessie slipped a pair of sandals on her feet and stowed her phone, keys, and wallet into the backpack before putting her arms through the straps and getting it situated comfortably on her back. She stepped out of her apartment door and set out through the courtyard and onto 2nd Avenue.

It was nearing lunchtime, and the street was full of tourists checking out the stores while they decided which restaurant they wanted to try for lunch. Nashville was famous for its Hot Chicken, and many places featured the spicy meal on their menu. The thought of it made Gessie's mouth water, but she resisted the temptation. She planned to pick up some cold cuts at the deli in the Urban Market and fix herself a sandwich when she got back to her apartment. It was the practical thing to do.

When Gessie had left her job out in California, she'd had a tidy nest egg. She had been able to save a good portion of her salary each year, and her investments had performed well. And Burton's controlling nature had ended up being a benefit in that area because he had seldom let her contribute toward household expenses. She'd assuaged her own guilt by buying Burton lavish gifts for his birthday, Christmas, Valentine's Day, or just as a surprise now and then. Even then, she didn't feel good about the arrangement, and what was worse was that toward the end, Burton had begun to complain if he felt the latest present hadn't exceeded the monetary value of the one before. It was a losing proposition all the way around.

Still, Gessie had a sizable portfolio when she'd left California, and she had decided she would allow herself one year to pursue her music without having to worry about a job. She had set aside enough money for the year to allow her to live comfortably, but not extravagantly. And she intended to stick to her plan. Eating out every meal would not fit in that plan. So, she tried to eat at home unless she was going out with Vanda or was too tired after busking and opted for take-out.

As she neared the corner of 2nd and Church, Gessie saw a small group of people watching a young woman who was one of Gessie's favorite fellow buskers. Unlike most of the buskers, this busker's performance didn't center around music. Sure, there was a boom box sitting on the sidewalk, blasting out music. However, the music was only there to provide the background rhythm for the busker's act, which was performing with hula hoops. The busker's name was Darla, and the fact that she was only twirling five hoops at the moment meant she was only about mid-way through her routine. Darla was adding another bright-colored hula hoop over her head when Gessie caught her eye. Gessie broke out into a smile, reached into the pocket of her jeans, and pulled out a $5 bill, which she flashed in the air and then deposited in the tip jar placed in front of where Darla was swirling the hoops. Just as Gessie knew she would, at the sight of the tip going into the jar, Darla gave an extra shimmy, twirled the newly added hoop in the air, and gave out a "whoop," before allowing the hoop to slide down her arm. Gessie gave a laugh, and walked on by with a wave, as Darla began to twirl the new hoop around her neck, while continuing to twirl the others she had around her chest and waist. Gessie had made a show of her tip with the hope it would encourage the tourists who were watching to make a similar contribution to Darla's jar.

Gessie never left her apartment without money for tips. It wasn't in her original plan because she hadn't thought about it before she began busking herself. While she was fortunate she didn't have to rely on tips, that was not true for other buskers on the street who counted on them.

CHAPTER 7

There wasn't much between 2nd and 4th on Church Street for tourists, except for the entrance to Printer's Alley between 3rd and 4th. But that was more of a nighttime destination. So, once Gessie turned the corner from 2nd on to Church, she had fewer tourists to contend with and didn't encounter any other buskers.

She picked up her pace and made good time over the last two and a half blocks. Once inside the door to the Urban Market, she reached down for a handbasket. When she stood back up and turned to begin her shopping, she ran right into Cole Trammel. Literally. Her head smacked right into the middle of his chest. She would have stumbled backward at that point if Cole hadn't instinctively put his arms around her to steady her.

It was awkward and yet nice at the same time. Gessie could hear Cole's heart beating, and she felt very safe and secure in his arms. It was a minute before she could speak. Was it just her imagination that Cole had seemed reluctant to let her go as she backed away? Come to think of it; Cole hadn't said anything either.

"Uh, I'm sorry," Gessie finally managed. "I didn't mean to bump into you. I mean, I didn't expect to run into you. I mean...Oh, for heaven's sake, I don't know what I mean. I'm babbling."

Cole had a mischievous grin on his face. "Are you stalking me, Gessie Chapel?"

Gessie gaped at him in shock. "What? Stalking you?" When her shock turned to anger, Cole put up his hands in mock surrender.

"Joke. I was just joking. Sorry."

They both just stood looking at each other for a moment. Neither of them seemed to want to leave but didn't quite know what to say. Gessie finally spoke up.

"Did everything go alright at the police station?" Gessie asked in a low tone.

The question caused Cole to do a quick survey of the store entrance to make sure there was no one nearby. "It went okay. I live right here. I'll tell you all about, but let's go up to my place."

A look of confusion crossed Gessie's face. "You live here at the market?"

Cole laughed and walked back to the nearby counter, where he picked up a couple of grocery bags.

"Actually, I live a few stories up. The market was one of the reasons I bought a condo in this building. It's pretty handy. I'd just finished checking out when I saw you come through the door. Come on, my building's entrance is right next door."

Gessie put the handbasket back in the stack by the door and followed Cole as he led her outside and then through the foyer of the building next door. They rode the elevator to the eighth floor and walked a short way to the door to Cole's apartment.

"This is nice," Gessie said as Cole ushered her inside. Like her apartment, Cole's condo was an open concept with the kitchen, dining, and living areas flowing smoothly from one to the other. Unlike Gessie's apartment, which was a bit outdated, Cole's condo was sleek and modern and more spacious, with a wonderful view of the city from the floor to ceiling windows that filled one side of the room.

"Make yourself at home," Cole said as he pointed to one of the chairs at the countertop that was part of the pass-through between the kitchen and the rest of the room. "Powder room is right over there if you need it. I just need to put these groceries away. I bought some chicken salad and some pita bread downstairs and was going to make myself a sandwich. Would you like to join me?"

"Deli was what I had in mind, too. I'd love to join you. Can I help?"

"Nope. This will only take a minute. Coffee, iced tea, water?"

Gessie said she'd love an iced tea. She slipped her backpack off and placed it on the floor next to her chair. She sat quietly as she watched Cole put away his groceries and then prepare the sandwiches. It was the first chance she'd had to get a close look at him. Of course, he was no longer in the running shorts and t-shirt she had seen him in early that morning. Now, he had on a light gray button-down collar shirt, with dark blue jeans and a pair of boots. On his belt was a large oval buckle with an American Eagle on it. The jeans fit him just right from Gessie's viewpoint, and the short-sleeve shirt showed off his tanned and muscled forearms.

Gessie tried to keep her mind from any further thoughts of just how sexy Cole looked. She was here to listen to how his day went. She didn't need a flush creeping up her cheeks that would let him know just what she was thinking when he turned around. She forced herself to take her eyes off Cole and instead looked around the living area of his condo. Her eyes settled on a guitar, leaning up against the end of the sofa. She let out an "Oh my!" and jumped off the barstool.

When she got to where the guitar rested against the sofa, she didn't touch it. She just knelt in front of it and studied it from every angle. She was looking at it so intently; she hadn't even heard Cole come out from the kitchen.

"Go ahead. Pick it up," Cole said from where he stood behind her.

"Oh, no. I couldn't. It's beautiful." Gessie paused and then added, "I've always loved the Gibson F-Hole guitar, particularly the ones from this era. It's from 1930, right?"

"You know your guitars, Gessie, and you can't hurt this one. It may be vintage, but it's meant to be played. And you can tell by the less than pristine finish that it's been played often. Come on. I can see you want to play it."

Cole picked up the guitar and handed it to Gessie. Gessie didn't even bother to get up. She cradled the guitar in her lap as she sat cross-legged on the floor. She did a tentative strum and then began picking out the intro to "Wildwood Flower."

"Ah, the Maybelle Carter scratch. I'm impressed," smiled Cole.

Gessie looked up and smiled in return. "It seemed appropriate with this guitar. It has a great sound." Gessie stopped playing and started to hand the guitar back to Cole.

"No. Not yet. You sing, too. Right? I didn't get a chance to hear you the other day when you were busking. Would you do a song for me now?"

A blush crept up Gessie's face. She didn't know why she was embarrassed. She'd been playing in front of strangers for over a month now. But somehow, this was different. It seemed intimate. She had to be careful what song she chose. She didn't want to sing one of her own songs. That seemed a bit pretentious to her. She also wanted to steer clear of anything that remotely sounded like a love song.

Cole had kept quiet and just sat patiently on the arm of his sofa, waiting for her to begin. Once she decided what to sing, there was nothing tentative about the way she played the intro to "Me and Bobby McGee." It had always been one of her favorite songs. She started with a slow, soulful tone on the first verse, adding a little more fervor and tempo as she went into the chorus. She was caught by surprise when Cole joined in on the second verse in flawless harmony. Cole dropped out after the second chorus and let Gessie finish out the repeat of the chorus and the fade-out to end the song.

Gessie was beaming when she ended the song. "Thanks so much for letting me play this wonderful guitar. I loved your harmony. That was fun!"

Cole took the guitar and then gave Gessie a hand up. "You're terrific, Gessie. Sorry, I jumped in there, but that's one of my favorite songs, and I just couldn't help it. I'm used to singing the lead. It was fun to do the harmony. Plus, we sound great together. We'll have to do that again sometime."

Cole had propped the guitar back up against the sofa and started walking toward the kitchen. Gessie wasn't sure if something about the song had reminded him of Gary, maybe it was because Gary had sung harmony, but he had gone quiet after his last comment. It had come out almost like a bit of polite conversation. Sort of like, when someone says they'll see you soon, but you never hear from them again. Maybe Cole needed to be alone.

"I'm sorry I got us distracted. Do you still want me to stay for lunch? I can leave if you have something else you need to do."

That seemed to snap Cole out of his thoughts. "What? No. Sorry. I was thinking about...Never mind. Let's have lunch. I'm starved. Then I'll tell you about my trip to the MNPD."

Cole set a plate in front of her that had a pita pocket stuffed with chicken salad. There was a piece of lettuce and a slice of tomato on the side, and a sprig of grapes. Once Cole had set another plate for himself on the counter, along with silverware, napkins, and two bottles of iced tea, he came around and sat on the barstool next to Gessie.

"Bon Appetit," Cole said as he added the lettuce and tomato into the pita and then took a big bite.

Gessie followed his example and began eating her sandwich. She decided it was her turn to be patient. Besides, she was perfectly content to sit beside Cole and remember how wonderful it felt to sing with him. Although she agreed they sounded good together, the music wasn't the only thing that was in harmony. Gessie felt the two of them were in harmony as well. She stole a look over at Cole, and he seemed to be deep in thought again. Even though he had said he wanted to talk, she was beginning to think she was intruding and should leave. She quickly finished the rest of her sandwich and popped a couple of grapes into her mouth, then stood up to take her plate into the kitchen.

"I'm being a terrible host," Cole said, jumping up from his chair as well.

"Don't be silly. I can't even begin to imagine what you must be going through. You probably need some time to yourself."

At this point, Cole had come around the counter, and Gessie had laid her hand on his arm as she spoke. She could see the anguish on Cole's face, and before she knew it, she had stepped in and put her arms around him. Sometimes a person just needed to be held, even if that person was a man who most likely wouldn't admit it.

Gessie could feel Cole's body relax as he put his arms around her, too, and rested his head atop hers. They stayed like that for several minutes before Cole released the hold and stepped away.

"I guess I needed that. It's all starting to hit me, I think. Gary used to be my best friend. I always thought we'd be able to mend fences at some point. Now that will never happen."

Gessie made a shooing motion and told Cole to sit back down. She'd noticed an espresso machine and a caddy next to it with coffee pods.

"I think I can figure out where everything is. You fed me. So, I'll clean up and make us some coffee."

"That sounds great, Gessie. Thank you."

As Gessie puttered around in Cole's kitchen, he began to fill her in on what had happened with Detective Warner. The detective hadn't been too happy to see Cole show up with his attorney. He was even less happy when the attorney wouldn't allow Cole to go into any detail about the lawsuit Gary had brought against Cole. Because it was clear the detective was only fishing, Cole's attorney had put an end to the interview fairly quickly. That didn't mean it hadn't been entirely unpleasant.

"Didn't you have to convince that detective that Gary was murdered?" Gessie asked. "Why would you have done that if you were the one who murdered him?"

"I know. This whole thing is crazy. They were going to just pass it off as an OD. Gary had been on drugs, sure. But he was hooked on pills. From everything I heard, the rehab was successful, and he wasn't taking those anymore either. I heard he was clean. Even if he had relapsed for some reason, he was afraid of needles. He would never have OD'd that way. Plus, Gary is left-handed. The needle was sticking out of his left arm, which means he would have used his right hand to shoot up. None of that fits."

A look of pain crossed Cole's face. Gessie was sure the scene from that morning was playing through his mind. It must have been horrible to find his friend that way. Gessie had finished making them each a mug of coffee, and she set one in front of Cole.

"So, did they find some evidence that made them start to agree with you?" Gessie asked.

"Well, I guess they did a notification to Gary's parents, and at some point, Mrs. Armbruster must have confirmed

Gary was afraid of needles. Mr. Armbruster went ballistic when the detective said I was the one who found Gary. He was the one who told Detective Warner about the lawsuit."

CHAPTER 8

Gessie had finished putting their dishes in the dishwasher, and when she came around the counter with her coffee, Cole suggested they move over into the living area. Cole sat on the sofa, and Gessie opted for a nearby armchair.

"I need to go back a little way to put this in perspective for you," Cole began. He'd already told her their high school band had broken up, but Gary and Cole occasionally got together and played a gig or two now and then. Mostly small parties, but they also played in a few of the bars around town that had open-air patios or other small venues that fit a duo better than a full band. The two of them had gone up to Tennessee for one of Spence's football games, and at the afterparty, they'd had a spontaneous jam session with Spence and one of his teammates who was the host of the party and a pretty good drummer.

Although Spence had been scouted for one of the pro teams, a nasty knee injury put an end to any thoughts of a football career. Spence had returned to Nashville after graduation and had started a music business. When Cole had graduated from Belmont, he had started teaching music at one of the schools in the area that had an acclaimed arts program.

Somewhere along the line, Cole realized he wanted to start up the band again. The problem was they needed a drummer, and although Gary lobbied for Buddy, Cole wanted no part of that. Spence solved the problem by asking his former teammate if he was interested in a move to Nashville to be the band's drummer.

"Trey worked virtually as a programmer at the time, and it didn't matter where he lived. So, he jumped at the offer," Cole grinned. "Things went smoothly for a while, and the band was starting to gel. We were starting to get more gigs and becoming known around the area. It was getting to the point where we were going to have to think about giving up our day jobs and make a commitment if we wanted to focus on our music full time."

Cole said it was at this point, the problems began. Gary and Rhonda had been an on again off again kind of thing. As the band gained popularity, it seemed Rhonda was around more often. She'd show up to rehearsals with Gary and was trying to insinuate herself into the group.

"I thought Rhonda was just using Gary to stay in the limelight. She wanted to be an actress and had landed a few modeling gigs around town, as well as a small part in a musical put on by one of the theater groups here. If Gary was going to be in the spotlight, Rhonda wanted to be right there with him. Since we had nixed the idea of her being in the band itself, she somehow convinced Gary to suggest maybe the band could just happen to notice her in the audience and then invite her up to do a guest spot. Gary was uncomfortable broaching the idea to us. But he seemed to be even more uncomfortable about the fact he was going to have to tell Rhonda the idea was shot down. Gary began missing rehearsals, claiming he couldn't get off work or that Rhonda needed him to accompany her to something or other. Rhonda was bad enough, but I also wouldn't have put it past Buddy to purposely try to cause problems for the band by keeping Gary at work. It was just the sort of thing he'd do because we hadn't asked him to be our drummer. Not that he wanted to be or even had the time to do it. He was just ticked we didn't ask him."

Cole said he had let it slide at first, and he would often work alone with Gary to go over any new material and make sure he was ready for their next gig. During those sessions, Gary was almost like his old self, and he and Cole could joke and talk with each other like they had since they were kids.

One night while they were hanging out at Cole's place, Gary had drunk one too many beers and passed out on Cole's couch. Cole had thought it best just to let him sleep it off. Cole hadn't had as much to drink, and he was restless. So, he picked up his guitar and quietly started working a song that had been rolling around in his head for a couple of days. He'd lost track of time, and at some point, Gary had stirred on the couch.

"That sounds great, man," Gary had said as he sat up on the couch. "Let me grab a beer, and I'll write it down for you."

Cole hadn't realized Gary had been awake and was even more surprised he seemed relatively sober. He'd suggested Gary have some coffee instead of another beer, but Gary had cited the old "hair of the dog" reasoning. Cole had shrugged it off, knowing Gary wouldn't listen to him anyway. True to his word, Gary came back with a beer and picked up the pen and pad of paper Cole always had handy. Cole sang through the song a few more times, while Gary wrote down the notes and lyrics, revising what he was capturing as Cole changed a note or a word as he repeated the song. When it was finished, there were two pages of the handwritten song, complete with scratched out words and notes that had been replaced with those that had ended up in the final version.

"That original version was right in line with the saying that all you needed for a country song was three chords and a guitar," Cole chuckled. "I was using a simple chord progression in the Key of G. Gary has a great ear and is a natural musician, and what he wrote on those two pages was what I had come up with that night. It wasn't until Matt picked it up and worked with it, however, that it became the song it is today."

Not long after that night, Gary had started to change even more. He was jumpy, forgot lyrics, and sometimes barely made it on time for their gigs. One week, he had missed two rehearsals, blown off Cole's offer to work with him on the side, and then had shown up not only late, but stoned for a gig. Cole had suspected Gary was on drugs and had tried to talk to him about it. Gary had, of course, denied he was on anything, and Cole had wanted to believe him, and so had Spence. But eventually, it became clear Gary had problems, and he wasn't going to be reliable.

"The rest of us in the band took a vote, and we decided we had to kick Gary out," Cole added softly. "Spence offered to tell him or at least be with me when I told him, but I felt like it had to be me. When I did it, Gary looked at me like I'd punched him in the gut. He walked out of my condo, and I hadn't talked with him since. I tried to call him many times to see how he was doing, but he wouldn't take my calls."

Cole's tone as he had talked about Gary was very somber but brightened slightly when he began to talk about Gary's replacement. After Gary had left the band, they needed someone to replace him, and Cole got in touch with one of his classmates from Belmont. By day, Matt Harrison had been the music director for a large church in the area. He had jumped at the chance to join the band for what they all thought was just a side job. That didn't last too long, however.

One of the first things that happened when Matt joined the band was that he saw the song Cole had written and convinced him he should cut a single of it. Matt was practically a savant at musical arrangement, and he had taken Cole's song to the next level as far as Cole was concerned.

"I took some composition courses at Belmont, and I'm pretty good at it if I do say so myself," Cole added. "But I can't hold a candle to Matt. He took one look at "Tired of Leaving," and it's as if he could hear the subtle difference adding a Gmaj7th or 9th would make, and his arrangement for the instruments and the vocals was something I wouldn't have been able to do myself."

The band had taken a vote after the release of "Tired of Leaving" and decided to call themselves the Cole Trammel Band. Cole had objected, but Spence, Trey and Matt had outvoted him. With the success of the hit single, the band began to get more and more booking requests, and it became clear they needed to make a decision about the band's direction. They surprised each other when, to a man, they all said they would be willing to quit their "day" jobs and focus on the band.

"The rest, as they say, is history," Cole said with a half-smile. "It may be my name on the band, but it's Matt who's the glue. He has a knack for knowing what works and what doesn't."

Cole seemed to drift off for a moment, and Gessie had to prompt him a bit.

"So, the lawsuit?"

"Oh, right. Sorry. I forgot that was where I was going with the story. When "Tired of Leaving" began to get some play on the radio, Gary sued me, claiming he had co-written the song with me. The lawsuit also claimed that I had kicked Gary out of the band in an attempt to hide the fact Gary had a part in creating what turned out to be a hit single."

"So, isn't it just your word against his?" asked Gessie.

"Well, there is the fact that I have the original pages of music. Gary knows me well enough to figure I would have kept them. The original music would clearly show they are in Gary's handwriting. While he was only copying down what I was playing and singing, it would give a lot of credence to his claim. So far, my attorney has stalled the proceedings, saying I haven't been able to locate the original version of the song. It's the version that Matt edited and arranged that was recorded, and that has no trace of Gary's handwritten version."

Cole paused again, and a look of such sadness crossed his face that Gessie couldn't help but reach over and take Cole's hand. "You don't have to say anything more. I can see how much this is hurting you."

"No, really, it helps to talk about it. You're nice to sit here and listen."

Cole released Gessie's hand and said he needed to get some water and asked if Gessie would like a bottle as well. When Gessie said she would, she followed Cole back toward the kitchen. She sat back down on her chair at the kitchen island, and took the bottle of water Cole handed her. After chugging about half of his bottle of water, Cole moved back out into the living area and began to pace as he went on with his story, saying things began to go from bad to worse for Gary. Gary had gone into a tailspin and started using drugs heavily. It had gotten so bad Buddy had even had to fire him.

With nowhere else to go and no means of support, Gary had moved back in with his folks, but had made their lives a living hell. He'd stolen money from them and gotten picked up for petty theft, all so he could buy more pills. One night they'd found him unconscious, and he'd been taken to the ER where they'd pumped his stomach. It had been a wakeup call for him, though, and his parents had convinced Gary to go into rehab. He had been in rehab while Cole and his band had been on tour.

"My attorney told me I couldn't have any contact with Gary with the lawsuit going on, but I tried to talk with him anyway. I just couldn't figure out why Gary would sue me. He knew all he did was copy down the words and music for me. I thought if I could just talk to him, we could work out whatever was really behind Gary suing me. But Gary's folks always answered the phone. They wouldn't let me talk with Gary, and they would immediately hang up on me. That hurt almost as much as Gary not talking to me. I guess it shouldn't have surprised me, though. It's just that their house was almost a second home to me when I was a kid. They stopped talking to my folks, too. But some mutual friends told them the Armbrusters blamed me for Gary turning to drugs and, of course, believed their son over me when he said I cheated him out of credit for co-writing "Tired of Leaving."

Cole stopped pacing, and his shoulders slumped.

"He called me that night before he died."

"What?" Gessie asked in surprise. That was something Cole hadn't told her before.

"He wanted to talk to me. He said he was sorry, and he was going to drop the lawsuit. He sounded good. Sober. I was so glad to hear from him and told him that I'd missed him. I told him I'd meet him anywhere, anytime, and that was what was important to me, not some lawsuit. I told him I'd planned on a morning run along the riverfront and suggested he meet me for breakfast. He laughed. Man, he had a great laugh. And he said I should know he wasn't a morning person. We used to always get cravings for Hot Chicken, and Gary suggested we meet up at Hattie B's tonight, for old times."

Gessie thought for a minute about everything Cole had told her. Then she asked, "Did you tell Detective Warner what you just told me?"

A flash of anger crossed Cole's face before he answered. "Yeah, I told him. For what little good it did. He kept hammering on the lawsuit and how I must have been even angrier about it now that the band is becoming famous. He turned the whole phone call around and said it was just my word that Gary said he was going to drop the suit. Instead, he accused me of threatening Gary to drop the suit. Hank, that's my lawyer, shut him down and told Warner he had no evidence I was involved in any way and that we were leaving. Warner didn't try to stop us, and Hank said that was because the detective was just posturing, trying to goad me into saying I had killed Gary."

An image of Detective Warner's piercing blue eyes flashed in her mind. She suspected Cole had gotten a glimpse of the intimidation she thought Detective Warner could summon if he so chose. "It's like you see on those TV dramas where they do a 'good cop, bad cop' routine on someone to get them to confess."

"Except, with me, there was no good cop," sighed Cole. "The one thing I did find out is the coroner places the time of death around midnight, and anyone could have found Gary between that time and when I jogged by. It would have been stupid on my part to take that risk if I had killed him and wanted to make it look like I stumbled upon him the next morning by accident."

"Well," Gessie said, "if the murderer is aware of the lawsuit and your connection with Gary, they must be congratulating themselves that it was you who found Gary."

"You're probably right; they'll be even more ecstatic once they learn I'm currently the number one suspect."

Just then, Gessie heard the words and music for Alice Cooper's "School's Out," and Cole walked over to a small table and picked up his cellphone, telling Gessie it was Spence and he needed to take the call.

Gessie didn't want to intrude on Cole's phone call. So, she decided it would be a good time to use the powder room. When she came back out into the room, Cole had finished the call and was just standing in the middle of the room. He looked so sad, Gessie couldn't help herself. For the second time that morning, she just walked over and put her arms around Cole.

"Are you alright, Cole?" Gessie murmured as she laid her head against Cole's chest and ran her hand, soothingly up and down Cole's back as she held him.

Cole had put his arms around Gessie and kind of sagged in her embrace. It was a minute or so before Cole seemed to gather himself, and he stepped away from Gessie slightly. He raised a hand and gently brushed back a strand of hair that had fallen across Gessie's face.

"You must think I'm a basket case. I can't seem to get my head around what's happened, and it just keeps getting worse. That was Spence. I had called him earlier and told him what had happened, and he went over to talk to Gary's parents. They'll still talk to him, and I asked him to give them my condolences. They not only didn't care to hear from me, they told Spence to make sure to inform me I wasn't welcome at Gary's funeral."

"Oh, Cole, I'm so sorry."

Cole's cellphone rang again. This time the ringtone was the chorus from "Angels," a song done by Randy Travis about mothers being angels on earth. A bittersweet smile crossed Cole's face as he stepped away from Gessie to answer the phone.

"Hi, Mom," Cole said softly. "I guess you heard."

Gessie took that as her queue to leave. She walked over and picked up her backpack from the floor and motioned to Cole that she was leaving. He asked his mother to hold on a minute and walked over to Gessie.

"I can't thank you enough, Gessie. I'd like to see you again after I get my head screwed back on right. Can I call you?"

"Of course," Gessie assured Cole. "You just take care of whatever you need to and let me know if there is anything I can do to help." She stood up on her tiptoes and gave Cole a quick kiss on the cheek and then went out the door as Cole turned to go back to his call with his mother.

CHAPTER 9

After Gessie left Cole's condo, she made quick work of her shopping at the Urban Market. She slipped on the now full backpack and walked back down Church Street at a leisurely pace. When she turned the corner onto 2nd, she could see Darla was gone, but she had been replaced by two young men she had never seen busking before. One was playing the harmonica, and the other was playing a mandolin. They were doing an instrumental of the bluegrass classic, "Wabash Cannonball."

Gessie listened for a minute and then reached into her pocket and pulled out another five-dollar bill. She smiled at the duo, gave them a thumbs-up, and then dropped the money into the large tin can positioned at their feet. The harmonica player incorporated an enthusiastic train whistle sound, giving out a musical "woo-woo" for Gessie's tip. Gessie laughed and gave them a wave as she walked the rest of the way down 2nd and went through the door to the courtyard for her apartment complex.

After putting away her groceries, Gessie was at a loss for what to do. She was upset. She was fortunate that she had never lost anyone close to her and couldn't imagine what Cole was going through. The only thing she did know was that she somehow wanted to make his pain go away. Gessie made herself a mug of coffee and went and sat down on the sofa. Almost on automatic, she reached for the remote and clicked on the TV.

As she sipped her coffee, she surfed through the channel guide, looking for a diversion more than anything. She was scrolling through the listings, when her eyes were drawn to the popup window running a commercial for the Buddy Norman Autoplex. "Come on down, and I'll drum up a deal for you!" shouted Buddy Norman as he launched into a drum solo.

Gessie clicked off the TV and jumped up from the couch. She knew exactly what she was going to do. She raced up the stairs to her bedroom and went into her walk-in closet, pushing aside hangars until she found what she was looking for. She pulled out the Rock & Roll Cowgirl blouse that had been a going away gift from a friend of hers who insisted it would be the perfect thing to wear in Nashville.

The truth was Gessie had never worn it. It was a creamy white off-shoulder blouse that had a ruffle around the top, embroidered with Aztec and floral designs. The problem was it showed more cleavage than Gessie was usually comfortable with, and it required a strapless bra. No way would Gessie not wear a bra. The irony was not lost on her that the strapless bra she had was also a push-up bra. So, there would be even more cleavage on display. Even though she knew she was going to be uncomfortable wearing the blouse, Gessie had already decided it was perfect for what she wanted to do. And that was to attract Buddy Norman's attention.

She took a quick shower and shampooed her hair. She took the time to blow-dry and then used the curling iron to style her hair so that her long blond hair would fall in soft, loose curls just below her shoulder. It would be a good look with the off-shoulder blouse. She didn't want to go overboard, but she also applied a bit more makeup than usual, finishing off with a mauve-colored lipstick.

After fitting herself into the strapless push-up bra, Gessie slipped on the off-shoulder blouse and a pair of skinny jeans and assessed herself in the mirror. "Hmmm, I think you could give Vanda a run for the money in the attention-getting department with this look," Gessie said to her image in the mirror. She had been afraid the outfit would come off as slutty, but that was not the case. Instead, she looked pretty.

Burton probably would have sneered at the outfit. It didn't have the level of sophistication he would have demanded of her if she had been on his arm. She decided she looked more like the sassy girl next door, and that made her smile. She was getting a little of her old confidence back, and she looked and felt happy.

Gessie made a mental note to take a little more time with her appearance in the future. She might play her music out on the street, but she didn't want to look like she lived there too. Humming the melody to Bob Marley's "Don't Worry, Be Happy," Gessie slipped her feet into a pair of Allbirds Breezers and then grabbed her backpack and transferred her wallet and phone into her tote bag and slung it onto her shoulder. She picked up her keys and headed out her door to the underground garage, where she had an assigned spot for her car.

It felt strange to be behind the wheel of her Audi. It was another remnant from her life in California that she didn't have much need for now. Pretty much everything Gessie needed was in walking distance. So far, she had only used the car for a once a week trip to the supermarket to pick up items either too bulky or too heavy to carry in her backpack after a trip to the Urban Market. The Audi was a large sedan, and it was tricky maneuvering it in the underground garage. It made perfect sense for her to be looking for a new car. And who could blame her for choosing the dealership advertised night and day on TV? There was no reason anyone would suspect her main goal was to get a look at the dealership's owner.

Gessie headed down Broadway toward Midtown. There was the usual downtown traffic, but Gessie wasn't in any particular hurry. She figured it would be a couple of hours before Vanda would be calling about meeting up for dinner.

The Buddy Norman Autoplex was pretty much what Gessie had expected. Rows upon rows of automobiles as far as the eye could see. There were three buildings set back on the lot that looked to take up a full city block. One building seemed to be for used auto sales and the dealership's service department, where the other two were for new car sales. It looked like one-stop shopping for either an American-made or foreign-made car from low-end to luxury. Take your pick. Gessie opted for the middle building, mostly because business seemed to be booming, and customer parking spaces seemed to be at a premium. So, she took the first one she spotted.

Gessie stepped out of her car and did a slow turn as she surveyed the lot. By the time she had turned back toward the building, a young woman was coming out a set of double doors, calling out a greeting as she walked quickly up to Gessie, extending her hand.

"Welcome to Buddy Norman Autoplex, where we'll drum up a deal for you. I'm Rhonda. What kind of automobile are you looking for today?"

Gessie was stunned. The woman in front of her looked nothing like the sexy girl in the commercials. She looked ten years older than what Gessie knew her to be. What had been a youthful face now looked haggard, and it was obvious she'd had some work done to her body. The enlarged breasts didn't seem to go with the rest of her shape, which Gessie would describe more as gaunt rather than slender. Rhonda had a smile plastered on a face that featured a little too much make-up. The smile looked forced as she extended her hand to Gessie.

As Gessie shook the woman's hand, she noticed there was a black armband attached around her right arm. For a moment, Gessie chided herself. Her initial thought had been that Rhonda had the look of a serious addict. But maybe what she was looking at was someone who was sincerely grieving.

"Oh my," Gessie pointed at the band. "Did I come at a bad time?"

Before Rhonda could answer, Buddy Norman walked over to the two women. Gessie had seen the man come out through the doors just a beat or two after Rhonda. She had recognized him immediately from the internet photos and the commercials. He must have heard Gessie's question and nodded at her, but he spoke first to the saleswoman.

"Rhonda, I'll take care of this young lady. You go on back inside and take it easy."

Several expressions seemed to flit across Rhonda's face; there was a mix of irritation, relief, and sadness. The first expression Gessie assumed would be the saleswoman in Rhonda who wouldn't like the boss taking away a potential sale, and the other two were probably because Rhonda's heart just wasn't in her work today. For a moment, Gessie felt terrible about choosing this day to scope out the dealership. Gary had worked here at one time. He was probably friends with many of the people who worked here, some better than others. Rhonda was one of those people who had known Gary well. It was to be expected she would be upset by his death. It did confirm one thing for Gessie. These people had all heard about Gary's death. With news available on-line 24/7, Gessie supposed she shouldn't be surprised.

Buddy Norman watched Rhonda as she turned and walked back into the building. There was no doubt in Gessie's mind that Buddy's gaze had everything to do with her body and nothing to do with her well-being. Rhonda may not have been the beauty she once was, but that didn't keep Buddy from leering at her. Gessie thought it was something Buddy did with any female. She was proven right when she saw Buddy's eyes rove over her own body as he turned back toward her.

"Hi, I'm Buddy Norman. It's true you've come on a sad day for us. We've lost one of the Buddy Norman family. But he was all about living each day fully, and he wouldn't have wanted his friends sitting around moping. Now, what kind of deal can I drum up for you today, pretty lady?"

"Wow," Gessie thought to herself. For someone who had known Gary since they were kids, she wasn't getting a sad vibe at all. She knew people handled their grief differently, but Buddy had just done a Dr. Jekyll and Mr. Hyde. True, he seemed sincere when he talked about Gary being a part of the dealership's family. Then, wham! The switch flipped, and he was back in sales mode and sleazy guy sales mode at that.

"OK. If you're sure it's not a bad time. I'm Gessie. I'm not sure what I'm looking for. I don't want some cracker box, but I do want something smaller than my Audi."

Gessie pointed at the Audi right in front of them, and Buddy asked her if she wanted to trade it in. When Gessie said she was open to that, you could see dollar signs in Buddy's eyes. The Audi was only a couple of years old and would still command a pretty penny on the used car lot. It was all about giving her the lowest trade-in value he could get away with and putting her in an upscale new car.

"I've got something I think you'll like," Buddy practically oozed the words as he gave her a sly side glance. There was clearly a sexual innuendo in his words, and Buddy had casually rested an arm at the small of her back to steer her toward the nearest row of new luxury cars.

Over the next half hour, but what seemed like an eternity to Gessie, she and Buddy went through a subtle dance of sorts where Buddy tried every trick in the book to put a hand on her. And Gessie did everything she could to thwart his attempts, while still seeming blissfully unaware of what was going on.

Gessie would sit in the driver's seat, and Buddy would reach across her to point out a feature. Before his arm could brush innocently across her breasts, Gessie brought her hand up, pointing to a push button on the steering wheel as if she'd just noticed it, effectively pushing his arm away in the process. He offered to help her in and out of the car. She politely declined. At one point, as they were walking toward a small SUV, Buddy reached out a grabbed her.

"Careful. Watch your step," Buddy called out as he pretended to steady her.

Okay, that was it. Gessie had had enough. She pushed him away and was about ready to give him a piece of her mind when a voice came over a loudspeaker.

"Buddy Norman to the sales floor. Buddy Norman to the salesfloor, please."

Initially, Buddy scowled. He didn't like being interrupted. But his self-importance won out, and he puffed out his chest. "I'm sorry. I'm urgently needed on the sales floor. I'll send Rhonda back out to help you."

Thankful for the reprieve, Gessie told Buddy sending Rhonda out wasn't necessary. She told him he'd given her a lot of options to think about, and she would make an appointment to come back and meet with him another day. She'd hated to say the words because she knew he would take them to mean Gessie was interested in him as well as his cars. The smug look on his face as he walked into the sales building, told her as much.

As Gessie walked toward her car, she noticed a silver sedan parked a couple of spots over. Gessie recognized it immediately as the type of car Detective Warner had pulled up in when he arrived at the Nashville Train Station to investigate Gary's death. She quickly turned her head away from the windows of the sales building and kept her head down as she unlocked her car door and slid into the driver's seat. She hoped Detective Warner was busy talking with Buddy Norman. Even if he had seen her, maybe he wouldn't recognize her. She looked a lot different than she had that morning when he had interviewed her.

She told herself there was absolutely nothing suspicious about her being at the dealership, and there would be no reason for the detective to wonder what she was doing there. The trouble was she didn't believe that. If Warner had seen her, he wouldn't like the coincidence.

Gessie crossed her fingers and then lost no time driving away from the dealership. She was driving back down Broadway when she got an idea. She checked her watch, turned onto 19th, and pulled into the parking lot near Hattie B's Restaurant. She dug her phone out of her purse and sent a text to Vanda.

"I'm at Hattie B's. The line's not too long. Are you finished with your meeting?"

Vanda responded almost immediately. "Be there in 15. Meet you in line or order me my usual."

While they were no longer in the midst of the tourist season, Hattie B's was still a popular place, and there was usually a line waiting to get in, especially this close to dinner time. From Gessie's experience, she judged it was going to be about a fifteen- or twenty-minute wait to get inside, which had limited seating indoor as well as out on a covered patio deck.

That was alright with Gessie. She passed her time in line by thinking about her experience at the autoplex. She hadn't learned anything that would help solve Gary's murder, but she did learn she now had her own reasons to dislike Buddy Norman. He was the type that thought no woman could resist him. In short, he was a creep. No wonder she got the vibe Cole didn't like him. She couldn't picture the two of them having ever been friends.

CHAPTER 10

Gessie was brought out of her thoughts by a flash of purple as it passed by her. "Vanda!" Gessie called out.

Vanda stopped in her tracks, turned, and then looked down the line of people. At first, her glance went right past Gessie, but as she came back down the line again, she looked straight at Gessie.

"Gessie? Is that really you?" Vanda asked. "I didn't recognize you. You look...amazing." Vanda paused, then added slowly, "Okay, what have you been up to?"

"Up to? Why do I have to have been up to something?"

They moved a few paces up and were almost to the door. Vanda hadn't said anything else and just gave Gessie a look that let her know she was still waiting for an answer.

"Okay. Fine. I decided to go out looking for a new car. I thought I should look like someone who could afford a new car and took a little more time with my hair."

"Uh-huh," Vanda started in a disbelieving tone. "And this new look didn't have anything to do with a certain country singer who was going into your apartment with you this morning?"

"What? No. Well, yes. Sort of. Look, it's a long story."

"Uh-huh," Vanda said again.

They'd gotten inside and waited another few minutes until they saw an empty table open up. They grabbed the table and put in their order. They both ordered the small platter of Hot Chicken with a side of southern greens and baked beans. The difference between the two of their orders was that the hottest Gessie could do was the "Medium, Warming Up" heat level, while Vanda ordered what they called the "Shut the cluck up, Burn Notice" level. They each ordered a beer and were waiting for their orders when Gessie looked up as the newest customers made their way inside the restaurant.

"What are the odds," Gessie mumbled mostly to herself.

That caught Vanda's attention, and she turned to see who Gessie was looking at. Vanda immediately stood up and waved at the two newcomers. Gessie watched as Cole Trammel saw Vanda waving at him. He nudged Spence, who was standing beside him, and they both started walking toward Vanda. When Vanda moved over slightly to make room, Cole saw Gessie for the first time. There was a brief look of confusion, then his eyes widened, followed by a big smile.

Gessie stood up so that she, too, could move over to make room for Cole and Spence to join them. Cole was looking at her, and it was obvious he liked what he saw. It wasn't at all the way Buddy Norman had looked at her, that had been more of a leer. No, when Cole looked at her, it was something else. She wasn't even sure she could put it into words. She just knew how it made her feel when he looked at her.

"Hi, Gessie, you look beautiful."

There it was. What Cole said sounded simple enough, but it made Gessie blush. People had told her before that she was beautiful, but they had just been words. She remembered when Burton had said those words to her, it was just another way of saying "Hello" and could have been followed almost immediately by something mundane like "Was there any mail?"

Vanda watched the exchange between Cole and Gessie and could see she was going to have to take matters into her own hands.

"I'm Vanda Dalton," Vanda said as she stood and extended a hand toward Spence. "I've met Cole, and I know you're Spence Appleby. Why don't the two of you join us?"

Cole seemed to remember his manners. "I'm sorry. Hi, Vanda. And Spence, this is Gessie Chapel."

Gessie had stood up and was shaking hands with Spence when Cole added, "I'm pretty sure she's stalking me."

Gessie's mouth dropped open, and her eyes went wide. It was only then she remembered Cole had told her he and Gary were supposed to meet at Hattie B's. But there had been no reason for Gessie to think Cole would still show up at the restaurant. Still, was that what had made her think of Hattie B's? She felt herself blushing again.

"Hey, I'm just kidding, and we'd love to join you."

Everyone sat down. As Gessie and Vanda's orders arrived, Cole and Spence put in their own orders. Gessie concentrated on her food and hoped that Vanda would forget about trying to find out what Gessie had been up to. At first, it seemed like she had lucked out because Vanda's attention was totally on Spence. Spence had noticed Vanda's menu choice and had complimented Vanda on having the good taste and courage to go for the seriously spicy chicken.

"Awesome," Spence had gushed as he'd given Vanda a fist bump and then ordered the same thing.

"Speaking of awesome, I saw you play," Vanda said to Spence.

Spence smiled and said he had seen her the night before when she and Gessie had been at The Stage, but she and Gessie had left before he could get Cole to make an introduction.

"No, I mean, I saw you play at Tennessee. You were outstanding. I was sorry when I heard you got injured."

Spence was surprised Vanda had been talking about his football days and not the fact she had seen the band playing the night before. He beamed at Vanda. "Uh, thanks. Yeah, my knee will never be the same. Things probably worked out for the best, though. I like what I'm doing now, and I get out of carrying any of the band's heavy equipment."

Vanda laughed, and she and Spence clicked the tops of their beer bottles together. Unfortunately, then Vanda turned to look at Gessie.

"So, Gessie, before these fine-looking men joined us, you were going to tell me what you were doing out this way. Since we've established your choice of Hattie B's wasn't so you would just happen to run into Cole, what was the real reason you were nearby?"

Gessie almost choked on the mouthful of chicken she had been chewing.

Cole started patting her on the back. "Are you alright?"

Gessie took a sip of her beer and was still glaring at Vanda when it dawned on her that Vanda had no idea what had happened this morning. She knew it would cast a pall over the meal, but it couldn't be helped.

"I can tell you about that later, but Vanda, there's something you need to know first. Since you were down in Franklin all day, you probably haven't seen or heard today's news. A friend of Cole and Spence was found dead this morning. Cole was the one who found him over by the Nashville Train Station. I happened to jog that way this morning, and I must have gotten there just after Cole did.

When you saw us in the courtyard this morning, we had just gotten through talking with the police at the scene."

Now it was Vanda's turn to sit there with her mouth hanging open. But only for a second. She immediately laid a hand on Spence's arm and spoke to both him and Cole.

"Oh, I am so sorry to hear you lost a friend. Did you know him long?'

When Spence said they'd all grown up together, Vanda's next question didn't surprise Gessie at all. Vanda had an innate ability to put people at ease, to say the right thing. This time was no exception.

"What was the craziest thing the three of you did together?"

The somber expression on Spence's face turned thoughtful for a moment, and then he laughed out loud as he looked over at Cole. Cole nodded his head and began laughing as well. When the two of them stopped laughing, they were using napkins to wipe the tears out of their eyes.

"Oh, man, I needed that," Spence finally managed to say when he had caught his breath. He looked over at Vanda and explained what the three guys had done. "There was another guy that hung out with us. But he was a relative newcomer to our group. Gary, Cole, and I had known each other since Kindergarten, but we only got to know Buddy when he transferred to our high school in our sophomore year. He was actually a year older than all of us. He said his parents had held him back a year so that he would have an advantage playing sports."

"It didn't matter," Cole interrupted, "since he wasn't good at any sports."

Spence chuckled, "Yeah, there was that. We all figured it had more to do with his grades. He wasn't good in that area either. Anyway, because he was older, he was the first one to get a car, and it was a beauty. Which figures since his dad owned several dealerships. It was a sweet ride, but he rarely let anyone else ride in it, even us, and we were supposed to be his best friends. It was Gary who had taken pity on the new kid nobody seemed to like and had brought him into our inner circle. Then one day, Gary was hopping mad. It seemed Buddy had finally let someone else ride in his car. Unfortunately, it was a girl Gary was crazy about. He thought he'd been making some progress and had just screwed up the courage to ask her out on a date, when Buddy swooped in and offered to give the girl a ride to and from school every day."

"It's an unspoken rule. You don't mess with a guy's car or his girl," Cole added.

Vanda was so intent on listening to Spence's story; she didn't notice Gessie kind of winced whenever Spence said Buddy's name. Gessie took a quick sideways glance at Cole, who also was enjoying Spence's story but was looking straight at her. And darn it, she could swear he sensed she was uncomfortable at the mention of Buddy's name. There was the briefest hint of a question in his expression before it returned to a big grin when Spence got to the good part of the story.

"Gary figured if Buddy messed with his girl, the appropriate method of revenge was to mess with his car. Gary's cousin had a friend who worked in a packaging store, and he sold us several large garbage bags full of those packing peanuts. We got them real cheap because someone had made a mistake, and the peanuts were pink, which a lot of customers didn't like, especially the male customers."

"Oh, boy, I think I can see where this is going," said Vanda.

"Yep, Gary's cousin picked up the bags and met us in the school parking lot the next day during lunch hour. Cole and I unloaded the bags while Gary used a slim Jim to pop the lock. Then the three of us got busy and crammed all those peanuts into the car. It was hard at the end to keep them from spewing out before we could get the door shut."

"It didn't help that we had to stop every few minutes because we were laughing so hard," Cole chuckled and then couldn't help but start laughing full-out again. That set Spence off too, and when he had finally stopped laughing, he told Cole to tell the end of the story so he could eat some of his chicken.

Cole nodded. "We all had history last period, including Buddy and the girl. I think her name was Melissa. So, it wasn't unusual that we'd all be walking out of the school at the same time. Gary, Spence, and I stayed a little bit behind, and there were several groups of kids in between us and Buddy by the time he and Melissa reached his car. Most of the other kids were upperclassmen, and Buddy always swaggered just a bit more because he was only one of a couple of other sophomores that had a car. He figured that alone made him an equal in the eyes of the juniors and seniors. So, it was doubly mortifying to Buddy when he and Melissa opened the doors to his car, and thousands of pink peanuts came streaming out. There must have been some static electricity going on, because some of what spilled out immediately attached themselves to Buddy and Melissa's clothes as well as in Melissa's hair.

"The juniors and seniors were howling. Melissa was screaming and swatting at her clothes and hair like she was being attacked by bees. The look on Buddy's face was priceless. And Gary..." Cole paused for a minute. "Gary just took it all in and then said, "Melissa's a bit crazy, don't you think? Looks like I dodged a bullet there."

This time everyone at the table laughed. "Did Buddy ever find out you all did it?" Gessie asked when she had stopped laughing.

"Nope," both Cole and Spence answered.

"What about Melissa?" asked Vanda. "What happened to her?"

"She wouldn't talk to Buddy after that. If he was anywhere near her and said something, she would look right through him as if he wasn't even there. People called her Pinky after that. She didn't like that much either. She went to college somewhere out of state. Her family moved some time ago, and I don't think any of them set foot in Nashville again."

Cole and Spence told a few more stories about Gary as they finished their dinner but then said they had to get moving. Although Cole didn't go into any detail, it sounded to Gessie like they were going to be looking up old friends to talk about Gary. She knew Cole was trying to find out if any of Gary's friends had been around him since he got out of rehab.

They had all managed to snag parking places in a nearby lot and walked together as they left the restaurant. They reached Gessie's car first.

"This is your car?" Cole asked as he looked at her car. "Funny, I don't see you as an Audi person."

That made Gessie laugh, and she asked Cole what an Audi person looked like. The look on his face told her he probably realized it was a question he shouldn't answer because nothing would sound right. Gessie let him off the hook. "Well, it's not the car for me any longer."

"That's what you were doing out this way," interrupted Vanda. "You were looking for a new car."

CHAPTER 11

Now it was Gessie's turn to sputter a bit. "Uh, well, yes. I thought I'd look at something a little smaller. This Audi is tough to negotiate in and out of our garage, and I walk almost everywhere these days."

"Hmmm," Vanda was mumbling to herself as Gessie continued to babble. "What's out this way. I've got it. You were at the Buddy Norman Autoplex."

It was like a lightbulb went off over Vanda's head. Neither Cole or Spence had mentioned Buddy's last name when they were telling the story about Gary, and there was no reason for Vanda to put anything together until now. She looked at Cole and Spence. "Wait a minute. The Buddy in your story was Buddy Norman?"

Spence told Vanda she was right, while a scowl came across Cole's face. "What are you doing, Gessie?"

Gessie looked like her hand had been caught in the cookie jar. Vanda was staring at her with a confused look on her face, and Spence had the same expression as he looked back and forth between Gessie and Cole.

"I...I," Gessie stuttered as she tried to come up with what to say. She was saved by having to say anything when Spence motioned to his watch.

"Cole, we need to go, or we're going to be late. Traffic is always bad this time of day."

Cole nodded that he'd heard his friend, but he kept his eyes on Gessie. "You need to stay out of this, Gessie. It could be dangerous."

Gessie knew Cole wasn't happy, and he wanted to say more, but the fact they needed to get going won out. "We are definitely going to talk about this," he said before turning to follow Spence across the parking lot where they got into a big Ford truck."

The truck rolled past them with Spence at the wheel, and it was only then Gessie noticed the big grin on Vanda's face.

"Ah, you like Spence, I see."

"What's not to like. Tall, handsome, and muscular, and he's got a great laugh. I gave him my number. But don't think you are going to get me off the subject of you and Cole Trammel. A whole lot is going on that I know nothing about. I've got a bottle of wine in my fridge that is just the thing to go with what sounds like what will be a fascinating story."

Gessie didn't even try to fight it. "Fine. As soon as I get home and change into something more comfortable, I'll be right over."

Vanda's car was already in the parking garage when Gessie pulled in, which wasn't surprising. Gessie had ridden with her a couple of times and knew that she had a lead foot. Plus, she knew the area a lot better than Gessie did and probably knew the best routes to take to avoid the downtown rush hour traffic.

Gessie hurried to her apartment and climbed the steps to her loft. She changed into a long tee and a pair of yoga pants and then brushed out her curls and pulled her hair back into a ponytail. She slipped her feet into a pair of flip flops, grabbed her phone and keys, and was back down the stairs and out her door in under fifteen minutes. Still, she wasn't surprised to see Vanda standing in her doorway, tapping her foot impatiently as she waited for Gessie to cross the courtyard.

"What took you so long?"

"I was just giving the wine time to breathe," joked Gessie.

"Ha. Good one." The frown on Vanda's face turned into a smirk. Both women knew the wine Vanda typically kept in the refrigerator needed no aeration. The fact that Vanda had said she had a bottle, however, indicated it might be a step above the boxed variety she usually had on hand. "Have a seat," Vanda pointed to the sofa.

Gessie made herself comfortable while Vanda went into the kitchen and then brought back two glasses of white wine.

"This is good," said Gessie taking a sip. "Trying something different?"

"If you must know, yes. I met a guy in the liquor department the last time I was at the market, and he talked me into a couple of bottles of this Chardonnay instead of my usual box. I have to admit I like it better and it doesn't cost all that much more. Now, no more stalling. You can start with why you were all dressed up to go car-shopping. You looked nice, by the way," Vanda added.

Gessie smiled at Vanda's last comment. "I have to admit it was kind of fun to get dressed up a bit. But the reason for that is way at the end of the story. It all started when I went out this morning for a jog along the riverfront."

Gessie proceeded to tell Vanda how she had gotten to the courtyard near the train station just after Cole had found Gary dead on one of the benches.

"I didn't get close, but the detective still interviewed me. When we were told we could leave, I asked Cole if he wanted to talk about it all."

"That was nice of you, Gessie. That's when I saw the two of you this morning. He filled you in on what happened to Gary."

"Well, not then." Gessie paused to get her thoughts in order. "He was still pretty shaken up then. He did tell me Gary was his friend and that it looked like he had overdosed. He didn't give me any details about how he OD'd, but Cole did say he didn't think Gary did it himself, and he had been quite insistent with the detective at the scene that at the very least, they should treat it as a suspicious death. This morning he talked mostly about how he had known Gary since he was a kid.

"Like you heard at dinner, Buddy Norman came along in High School. What he and Spence didn't talk about at dinner was that the four of them and a girl named Rhonda were in a band together. There was some tension within the group, and they broke up shortly before they all graduated. The other thing he told me was that Gary was in the Cole Trammel Band for a short time. He didn't tell me much more then because he got a call from the detective advising him that he needed to go down to the station for another interview."

Gessie told Vanda that after Cole left, she had gotten curious and had gone online to see what she could find out about the band, and that's when she'd found the articles about Gary suing Cole and how Buddy was quoted frequently speaking out against Cole. Those articles had then prompted her to do a search on Buddy Norman.

"Have you seen those commercials, Vanda? He's a real sleaze."

"So, what possessed you to go out to his dealership? Did you even see him?"

"Oh, I saw him alright, but that's getting a little ahead of the story. I didn't get the urge to go see the guy in person until I talked to Cole again."

"He did call you back later?"

"Not exactly."

Gessie described how she had literally bumped into Cole at the Urban Market.

"He had just gotten back from the police station, and he invited me up to his condo for lunch. He lives in that building."

"Oooh," interrupted Vanda. "I've been in those condos before. They're really nice."

Gessie couldn't help but picture Cole's condo, and she smiled at the memory of her and Cole doing the duet of "Me and Bobby McGee."

"What?" Vanda questioned, seeing the look on Gessie's face. "Something good happened. I want all the details."

"Vanda, the man was hurting. Nothing happened. He talked. I listened."

"You were smiling."

"Yeah, Cole has this amazing classic guitar. When he saw I had noticed it, he told me I could play it. I picked on it a little and then he asked me to sing something. The guitar was beautiful and had a great sound."

"But what did you sing? Was it one of your songs? What did he say?"

"Geez, Vanda. It was nothing. Well, not nothing. It was great. I sang, "Me and Bobby McGee.""

"Oh, that's one of my favorites, and I love the way you sing that," Vanda interrupted again.

"Apparently, it's one of Cole's favorites, too. He even joined in and harmonized with me on the chorus." Gessie paused, and then the expression on her face softened as she added, "We sounded really good together, and it took his mind off his friend for a few minutes."

Tears welled up in Gessie's eyes. "You should have heard him, Vanda. He is so sad, and he can't even go to his friend's funeral."

Gessie filled Vanda in about the lawsuit and how Gary's parents somehow blamed Cole for everything that had happened. They believed Cole had cheated Gary, and that was when he spiraled out of control. Gessie knew Cole wanted to find out more about Gary's rehab and how long he had been back home. He'd said when Gary's parents wouldn't talk to him, he decided he'd try to track down some of Gary's other friends to see if they could tell him if Gary had straightened out.

"I'm sure that's where Cole and Spence were going after they left Hattie B's. They were going to look up some old friends. I just want to help."

"Okay. So, that's what you were doing at the Buddy Norman Autoplex? Why him? What was your plan?"

"Well...," Gessie hesitated, "It sounded to me like Buddy and Gary had stayed friends, but they'd also had a falling out at some point. Maybe not a falling out. But Buddy had fired Gary at some point before he went into rehab. Maybe they'd mended fences recently. I don't know. I just wanted to get a feel for the guy. I got that for sure; I didn't like him at all."

"If you already thought you wouldn't like the guy, then why did you dress up to go out there?"

"Because you can tell by his commercials. He's also a major sleaze. I figured I'd have a better chance of him noticing me if I changed up my look a little."

"Like I said before. You looked stunning. Any man with a heartbeat would notice you. I take it Buddy was no exception."

"Buddy came right out to help me himself, shooing off the saleswoman who had originally approached me. And get this, the saleswoman was Rhonda. The girl that had been in the guys' band and she's also the girl in the Autoplex commercials you see on TV, at least the early ones."

Gessie told Vanda how all the employees were wearing black armbands, and Rhonda had told her it was because someone they had all worked with had died.

"Her eyes were puffy from crying, and she appeared to be shaken up. She might have also been strung out. I'm not sure. She looks a lot different than when she was doing the commercials. Buddy, on the other hand, looked like he had taken the news about Gary just fine and seemed more concerned about how good it made him and the dealership look for memorializing Gary than actually being affected by his death. And I was right about him being a sleazeball. He tried to cop a feel every chance he got. I was trying to work the conversation back around to Gary when Buddy was paged to return to the office."

Vanda's eyes got big when Gessie described how she had recognized Detective Warner's car in front of the building and hoped he hadn't seen her.

"I'm guessing you were going to feign ignorance and stick with your story about just being there to buy a car?"

"Well, Buddy did show me a couple of cars I liked, and I do think I'll buy a new one. I'd just never buy it from Buddy. I didn't learn anything about Buddy and Gary, but I don't think I'll be heading back there for another attempt. That guy is just too much of a creep."

"I can't see you leaving this alone. You've got something else planned. Don't you?"

Gessie gave a noncommittal shrug. She wasn't going to tell Vanda she had another idea she was going to check out. She had a feeling Vanda would have the same sort of reaction Cole had had earlier when he'd asked what she was up to. It was probably better neither of them knew what she was planning to do.

The wine was gone, and Gessie's big yawn more than hinted she was ready to call it a night. She thanked Vanda for the wine and walked across the courtyard to her apartment. The next day was Saturday, and she planned to be out on the street busking. She was itching to try out her new song on an anonymous and fluid audience. And after she was finished, she'd try and track down one of her fellow buskers who might be able to help her with her plan.

CHAPTER 12

Gessie slept in a little later than usual on Saturday. If she timed it right, she could run along the Cumberland River Greenway, cut over to the trail that led through Bicentennial State Park, and end up at the Farmer's Market when they opened at 8 a.m. She'd have to slow her pace on the way back since she planned to buy enough fresh peaches to make a pie. She thought if she strapped her backpack on tight enough, the peaches wouldn't bounce around and get bruised. Even if she ended up walking on the way back, that would be alright.

The last few days had been unseasonably warm. But this day had dawned crisp and clear, and the fall colors were on full display along the riverfront. Gessie had loved the weather in California, but as the summer months gave way to autumn, Gessie realized she had missed the change of seasons. Maybe she'd be singing a different tune when the winter snows began to fall, but for right now, she was happy.

The jog turned out to be just as enjoyable as she had anticipated, and when she inspected the peaches, she decided they had made it through the journey just fine. She had taken the precaution and walked on the way back, and none of the peaches appeared to be bruised. The seller at the Farmer's Market had asked if Gessie was making a pie. When Gessie said that was precisely what she was going to do the lady told her the peaches were almost ripe enough and gave Gessie a tip for speeding along the process if she wanted to make the pie the next day.

Once inside her apartment, Gessie took the peaches out of the backpack and arranged all but one of them inside a brown paper bag the market lady had given her along with the fruit. The lady assured Gessie if she let the bag sit out at room temperature, the peaches inside would be just right the next day for her to use in her pie.

Gessie had plans for the peach she had set aside, and she hurried upstairs to shower and change into the clothes she would be wearing when out busking later. Once she was back downstairs, Gessie poured herself a bowl of cereal and then peeled and pitted the peach. She then sliced the peach, and after popping the first slice into her mouth, she added the rest to her cereal. She savored the peach slice in her mouth while she fixed herself a cup of coffee. When it had finished brewing, she added milk to her cereal bowl and then sat at the kitchen counter to enjoy her breakfast.

The peach was juicy and flavorful, and she couldn't wait to make the pie the next day. Baking was something else she hadn't done for a while. Burton didn't like the mess he claimed she made in the kitchen, even though she always left it spotless. And while he ate the cake or pie she made, he always commented on it not being as good as such and such a bakery. "What in the world was the matter with me?" Gessie asked herself for about the thousandth time when she wondered what had possessed her to put up with Burton's mind games for as long as she did.

Once she'd finished her cereal and cleaned up her dishes, Gessie went to her guitar case and lifted out her Epiphone. So much had been going on that Gessie hadn't played it for a couple of days. She held the guitar like it was an old friend and began to check each string to make sure the instrument was in tune. As she made the final tweak to the bottom E string, she slid her fingers into position and began to strum a chord progression in the key of G.

She usually wrote her music in the key of C and wondered to herself why she was idly playing a G Major progression. Then she realized Cole's hit song "Tired of Leaving" was in G. She'd only heard the song a couple of times, but it had stuck with her. She wasn't surprised both Cole, and his song were on her mind. After all, she planned to do some snooping later in the day that she hoped would help Cole find out what happened to Gary.

Right now, however, she needed to work on her own song to make sure she was ready to give it a test run when she went out busking. She still had a little time before the early lunch crowd was out on the street, and she cleared her mind of everything else as she switched to the key of C and began to sing.

The words to her newest song came easily, and she was surprised when she realized she'd already passed the spot she had been unhappy with. She stopped abruptly and jumped up and went over to the end table where she'd left her handwritten copy of the song. She propped her guitar against the arm of the sofa, grabbed a pencil, and changed one of the chords in the second line of the song. It was a simple change from the major chord to a major 7th, but it made all the difference in the feel of the song for her.

She picked up her guitar and ran through the song again. This time she was conscious of the change she had made and, for the first time, was truly happy with the song she had created. She couldn't wait to get outside and see what kind of reaction she might get from the people who would stop and listen to her on the street.

Gessie put her guitar back in its case and then loaded up her backpack with what she would need with her while she was out busking. She had extra strings and some picks in the guitar case, but she carried some wipes, tissues, bottled water, and power bars in her backpack. She planned to stay close to home, but she still liked to be prepared. She set both the guitar case and her backpack by the door so she could grab both of them when she got back from the little errand she needed to take care of first.

She tore out a piece of paper from the tablet on the table and quickly wrote out a note. "If you can meet me in Butler's Run at 3:00 p.m., coffee and pralines are on me." Gessie folded the piece of paper and then scrounged around in her desk drawer until she found a paper clip. She clipped the note to a five-dollar bill and then put both into the front pocket of her jeans. She grabbed her cellphone and her keys and hurried out of her apartment and through the courtyard onto 2nd Avenue.

As she walked down 2nd toward Broadway, Gessie saw she was right that this beautiful Saturday morning would bring out a lot of people. There were more people than normal going in and out of the shops, and they would soon be joined by the early lunch crowd. Gessie picked up her pace. Before she could start performing, she needed to pass along her note to one of her fellow buskers.

She was looking for a busker named Gloves. He was an interesting guy. Gessie had made it a point to get to know the other buskers in her area. With Gloves, it had been a little more complicated than others. Gloves was a mime. He wore the iconic black and white striped shirt, and his face was covered in white pancake makeup with his facial features accented. He changed out the color of his pants and his hat and added red suspenders, occasionally. The one thing he kept constant besides the striped shirt was a pair of white gloves, hence the street name.

Gloves took his craft seriously and never spoke when he was in his mime costume. Never. Not even if he was taking a break or you happened to see him walking out on the street. But Gessie had discovered the mime had a sweet tooth, and when his day was over, he would go home, change out of his costume, and hit either the praline shop in Butler's Run or an ice cream shop a little further down 2nd Avenue.

Gessie had learned about Butler's Run the first morning she had gone out for a jog in Nashville. It was a shortcut between 1st and 2nd Avenue and was located at Commerce Street. The structures on either side of the walkway contained businesses and residences, and the entrance off 2nd was graced by a bronze statue of a dog that had once belonged to the owner of the breezeway and its buildings. The plaque on the base of the statue stated Butler was a shelter dog who took daily walks with his owner through the streets of downtown Nashville. Upon his death in 1999, the statue was created, and the walkway named in memory of the Spaniel/Labrador mix.

Just past the statue was a candy shop that featured world-famous pralines. Gessie had never had a praline until she had moved to Nashville. She immediately fell in love with the delicious confections, and it was during one of her own indulgences that a man approached her and asked if he could join her at the small table where she was sitting in front of the shop. Gessie hadn't recognized the man, but his tone of voice had made it sound like they were old friends. Gessie was about to refuse, when the man let out a laugh and then stopped dead still.

He set the coffee cup and small sack he had in his hands on the table. Before Gessie could object, he put his index finger and thumb together and, in an elaborate gesture, proceeded to act like he was zipping his lips. He then smiled broadly, bowed and did a gliding sidestep to the chair, pulled it out, swiped his hand across the seat as if he was dusting it off, and then sat down.

By this time, Gessie was laughing, and she gave a little clap. "Gloves! Yes, yes, please join me."

Gessie learned a lot about Gloves that day. The first thing was his real name was Devon Finkle, but he preferred Gloves. The funny thing was that while Gloves never said a word when he was in character, he talked a mile a minute when he was out of makeup. By the time they had finished their coffee and snacks, Gessie knew about Gloves's entire family and why he had become a mime. He had been precocious as a child and was just as talkative then as he was now. When he had done something bad, or he had just talked for so long his mother needed a break, she would have him sit in the corner with the added punishment that he could not talk.

Gloves had proceeded to teach himself sign language at the age of five and would continue to carry on conversations with himself as he sat in the corner. He also learned that he could avoid the corner if he found alternate ways to talk. That's when he began substituting gestures instead of simply asking his mother for something. A raised index finger to get her attention. Pretending to drink something if he was thirsty. A bow to say thank you. For her part, his mother knew she probably shouldn't encourage the pantomimes, but some days she just couldn't help herself and basked in the blessed silence.

Gloves found himself in the corner again when he went to elementary school, but now he had an audience. Behind the teacher's back, he kept his classmates entertained with various faces and gestures. Sometimes he was able to pass along an answer or two, and somewhere along the line, the entire first grade learned to communicate in sign language.

Gessie found Gloves fascinating, and since that first day, she would see him two or three times each week. The only person Gessie talked to more often than Gloves was Vanda. One of the things she learned from Gloves was that he knew a lot about what went on downtown. When he didn't have an audience, he tended to stand very still. It allowed him to observe everything and everyone around him.

Another thing about mimes was that, like clowns, they made a lot of people uncomfortable. That meant they were often avoided. Gloves had told her that when he was walking around downtown, most people tried not to make eye contact. It didn't seem to bother him, and once again, it allowed him to observe people without much, if any, interaction. If he had seen a person more than once, he could probably tell you where they worked or liked to shop, where they liked to eat and if they had any set routine.

Gloves was just the person Gessie needed to talk with to get the information she wanted. As she turned the corner on Broadway, she immediately spotted Gloves and smiled. He had a small audience around him. He was in the middle of his locked box routine, where he pulled out a big plastic key and asked one of the people in the audience to hold it for him. He made a big show of walking around an invisible box and then opening the door. Once he walked inside the box, Gloves made it clear by the expression on his face that the door had slammed shut behind him, and he went through several antics trying to get out. Eventually, it would seem to dawn on him that the audience member had a key, and he would frantically gesture at the person to use the key to open the door.

As always, the crowd loved the bit, and Gessie was happy to see everyone was digging into their pockets to leave a tip. Gessie chose that moment to catch Gloves's eye as she flashed the front and back of her note and tip as she added it to what the others had put in the upturned top hat Gloves used for his tip jar. With her mission accomplished, Gessie hurried back to her apartment, picked up her guitar and backpack, and went back out on to 2nd Avenue to take up her favorite busking spot, right outside the entrance to her apartment's courtyard.

Gessie performed until a little after one in the afternoon. There had been quite a bit of traffic in front of her spot throughout the lunch hour. As usual, she had done a mix of country favorites and her own music, and she had been more than pleased with the response she had gotten to her new song. Feeling like it had been a good day, Gessie packed up her things and then headed to her apartment.

She fixed herself a sandwich and then went upstairs to shower and change. She wanted to make sure she was in front of the candy store in plenty of time to meet with Gloves.

CHAPTER 13

Gessie had only been sitting at a small table for about five minutes when she saw Gloves entering the Butler's Run breezeway from 2nd Avenue. As was his custom, Gloves gave the statue of Butler a quick pat on the head as he walked by, and then he hurried to greet Gessie. No matter how many times she had seen him, the change in Gloves from his mime persona to his real nature never failed to amaze her. Without his makeup, Gloves had features that were best described as average. Not handsome, but not ugly either. He had an average face, an average build. But there was one overwhelming difference. Restless energy practically vibrated the air around him. He seldom stood still, and when he spoke, he spoke in run-on sentences.

"You look great, Gessie. I was so happy you wanted to get together this afternoon. You don't have to treat me, you know. I probably would have been headed over here today anyway. It was a good morning. Lots of folks. Not too many scaredy-cats. Pretty good tips." Gloves said all this as Gessie stood up to meet him, and they exchanged a hug.

When Gloves paused for a breath, Gessie linked her arm with his and steered him into the praline shop where she ordered each of them two of Leon's Classic Pecan Pralines and a cup of coffee. They took their candy and coffee back out to the table in front of the store, and Gloves began talking as soon as they sat down.

Gessie listened with amusement as Gloves regaled her with stories about the people who had watched him performing on the street over the last couple of days. Like clowns, many people did not like mimes. Some were even afraid. They were the ones Gloves referred to as scaredy-cats. They were easy to spot because it was immediately clear they were watching Gloves because someone they were with made them do it. Left on their own, the scaredy-cat would have crossed the street to avoid Gloves at all costs. He'd been doing his act for long enough that he knew the difference between someone who didn't like mimes versus someone who was just afraid. He didn't push too hard, but Gloves had told her he tried various ways to draw the scaredy-cat into his act. He was extremely pleased with himself when he felt he had been successful and turned a scaredy-cat into at least a reluctant fan.

After several minutes where Gloves paused in his storytelling only to take a bite of a praline and a sip of coffee, he sat back in his chair and made a motion like he was dusting off his hands. It was almost like he was giving himself a signal to change from one personality to the other.

"Okay, lovely lady. I can be quiet if I think about it. I thank you for the coffee and treats, but I know you had a reason you wanted to meet with me since you made a special point to leave me an invitation this morning. Is there something I can help you with?"

Gloves gave Gessie a look of such concern that she couldn't help but imagine his face in white pancake makeup. While Gloves could barely sit still and talked a mile a minute when he wasn't in character, he managed somehow to keep his face almost expressionless. For him to show any emotion, meant he was truly worried about the reason Gessie had requested they meet. Gessie would have liked to put him at ease, but she was pretty sure what she was about to ask him would do just the opposite.

She started by asking Gloves if he had heard about the man found dead over by the train station. When he replied that he had, Gessie went on to tell him she had been there shortly after Cole Trammel had discovered the body. She wasn't surprised when Gloves told her that he knew of both Gary Armbruster and Cole Trammel. Gloves had lived in Nashville all his life and was a walking encyclopedia about the city and its people, especially performers. It didn't matter if they were a busker or an international star, Gloves could probably tell you something about each of them.

"So, Gloves," Gessie started tentatively, "Gary Armbruster had a drug problem." Whether consciously or unconsciously, Gloves was nodding at Gessie's statement. It might have just been a result of Gloves's continuous body movement, but Gessie took it as a good sign that Gloves was aware of Gary's drug usage.

"But Gary had gone into rehab. He called Cole the night before he died, and Cole got the impression he was clean. From what Cole said, it sounded to me like Gary was going through part of the twelve-step plan. Cole doesn't think Gary overdosed, and even if he had, he wouldn't have chosen to do it with a needle."

Gloves was still nodding, and since Gessie had paused, he started talking.

"Knew about the drugs and the troubles between Gary and Cole. Knew Gary was out of rehab and living in a sober living residence not far from here. Not supposed to know, but there's a local Narcotics Anonymous group that meets in one of the church basements a few blocks from here. I happened to see Gary go in a couple of times in the last few weeks."

Gloves paused, and he looked at Gessie. Gessie knew it was time to let Gloves know why she had wanted to meet with him.

"I want to help Cole. The police consider him a suspect, and he wouldn't have done anything to hurt Gary. He was over the moon that Gary had called him and wanted to get together. Gary even said he was going to drop the lawsuit. I know you know a lot about everybody downtown, and I was wondering if you could point someone out to me who sells drugs."

Gloves frowned. "Why do you want to be messing around anybody like that?"

Gessie explained that she was hoping to find out who Gary's dealer used to be. "I figure if Gary did relapse, then he would have gone back to his usual source. If he didn't, then the odds increase that he didn't relapse, and someone killed him and tried to make it look like he had done it himself."

"Won't give you a name. Too dangerous for you, and they wouldn't talk to you anyway."

"But...," Gessie interrupted.

"I'll ask around."

"No. No," said Gessie. "If you think it's too dangerous for me, it's too dangerous for you, too. Forget I said anything."

Gloves nodded but didn't say he'd drop it. Instead, he thanked her for the coffee and pralines, and told her the next time it was his treat.

Gessie stayed where she was for a few minutes, thinking over her conversation with Gloves. While she hadn't gotten a name like she'd wanted, she had learned a couple of things. If she could figure out where the recovery residence was or which church might be the one that had NA meetings, she might be able to find someone who knew Gary and would talk to her. With her being so new to Nashville, she knew it wouldn't be easy for her to figure out where either of those places were, but she knew someone who might.

Pulling out her cellphone, Gessie sent a text to Vanda. "Pizza at my place tonight at six?"

Vanda's return text was, "I'll bring the wine."

Since Vanda worked freelance, it was her own decision as to whether or not she wanted to meet with a client over the weekend. But she often did just that because it showed a potential client she was placing them first. When Vanda showed up at her door promptly at six, she looked wrung out. With barely a "hello," Vanda went straight to the kitchen where she pulled a corkscrew out of a drawer, opened the bottle of wine, poured both herself and Gessie a glass, and then took a gulp from her glass as she extended the other to Gessie.

"Wow, I needed that," Vanda said as she plopped down on one of the stools at the counter that separated the kitchen from the rest of the apartment's living area.

"Hello, to you, too. Difficult client?"

"Worse," Vanda replied. "My mother. Don't get me wrong. I love her. But she wears me out both mentally and physically. Between the marathon shopping and the non-stop third degree about my love life and my failure to make her a grandmother, I'm exhausted. Here it is Saturday night, and I have no energy to go clubbing. Hopefully, this wonderful sauvignon blanc will jump-start me enough so that I'll at least be able to lift the pizza to my mouth and chew."

As Vanda finished her mini-rant, the doorbell chimed, and Gessie went to claim their pizza from the delivery boy, or in this case, the delivery man, who looked to be on the downhill side of forty and who'd sampled his fair share of his company's product. But he was pleasant enough and seemed to appreciate the tip Gessie gave him. So, they both came away from the exchange in a good mood.

Gessie had already put out plates, silverware, and napkins on the island countertop, and she now placed the pizza box squarely in the middle between her and Vanda. Both of them dove into the pizza, and neither said a word for a few minutes. The wine and the delicious pizza had restored Vanda somewhat. On the one hand, Gessie thought that was a good thing. She hated to see her usually energetic friend so drained. But on the other hand, Vanda was now giving her a look Gessie knew all too well.

"Don't look at me like that."

"You mean I shouldn't look at you like you are doing something that you shouldn't be. You already went way out on a limb snooping around the car dealership. What's going on in that head of yours? Start talking."

"I don't know. I've been thinking about the lawsuit. I know Gary is from Brentwood and although it's one of the nicer suburbs from what you've told me, I don't think the people are super-wealthy, and it didn't sound to me like

Gary's lifestyle was one that would allow him the money he'd need for an attorney for that kind of case. Those things can drag out. I can see his parents coming up for the money for his rehab, but it seems unlikely they'd be the ones paying the attorney for the lawsuit. Because Buddy was always quoted in the articles about the lawsuit, I wondered if maybe he was the one who had given Gary the money for that."

"Okay, but even if that's the case, what's that got to do with Gary's murder?"

Gessie sighed. "I have no idea. Maybe nothing. If Buddy was paying for Gary's legal fees, Buddy must have had a soft spot for him. But he also ended up firing him. I just can't get a clear picture of Buddy. Then there's Rhonda. I'd like to know more about her relationship with Gary. I thought I'd try to learn a little more from Cole the next time I talk with him."

"That's all interesting, but I still don't see why you care about the lawsuit. It seems to me that's the last thing you want to draw attention to. After what you've just told me, only Cole would have a motive if the murder was because of the lawsuit."

Gessie was nodding her head. "I can't disagree with you, and I hate that. It just you never know how one thing influences something else. Anyway, I don't know when I'll talk to Cole again, so I thought there was another way to approach this. If we could find out if Gary had relapsed or where he got the drugs, maybe that would lead us to who murdered him."

Gessie lowered her head, but Vanda stiffened with alarm. "Oh no, Gessie, what else did you do?"

CHAPTER 14

Gessie told Vanda about her meeting with Gloves and managed to keep her from going off the deep end by getting quickly to the part where Gloves had refused to give her the names of any drug dealers. Vanda gave a sigh of relief and gave her friend a stern look.

"Well, at least someone has some common sense. What were you thinking, Gessie? You don't know this town. There are some dangerous places and even more dangerous people."

Gessie didn't mention to Vanda that Gloves had told her he'd see what he could find out for her. Instead, she casually mentioned Gloves had told her there was a recovery residence somewhere close to downtown, and he knew that's where Gary had been living.

"Gloves also said one of the churches nearby held AA and NA meetings, and he had seen Gary at that church."

Vanda interrupted, "Don't even think about it."

"What? I just thought I could talk to some people who might know whether or not Gary was having any problems staying clean."

"And you thought you could just waltz into the recovery residence or pop into an NA meeting and everyone would just open up to you? The Anonymous is in the name for a reason. Please don't tell me you're planning to pretend you're an addict?"

Vanda's voice had gotten louder, and she was glaring at Gessie, shock on her face. "Why are you getting involved in this? Let the police handle it."

Somewhat deflated, Gessie shrugged her shoulders and looked at her friend. "After Cole convinced the police to look at Gary's death as a murder, they seem to have focused on him as the primary suspect. I don't think they're looking too hard at anyone else. I know I've only known him for a couple of days, but it feels a lot longer than that. I really care for him, Vanda. I want to help him. If I can find out a little more about Gary, maybe it'll be something that would lead to Gary's killer."

Seeing she wasn't going to be able to talk her friend out of getting involved, Vanda softened her tone. "Okay. I'm guessing you think I might know the location of the recovery residence and the church that has the NA and AA meetings. Sorry, I don't." Seeing the dejected look on Gessie's face, Vanda hurried to add, "But an old friend of mine used to go to meetings."

"Can we call your friend?" interrupted Gessie.

"No," Vanda said. "My friend moved away a few years ago, and we've lost touch. There are several churches here downtown that might hold the meetings. I doubt she would have told us which one even if I did call her. But I ran into her a couple of times at a coffee shop over on 4th. She'd acknowledge she'd seen me, but she never introduced me to the people she was with. After about the third time it happened, she finally told me they were people from her NA meeting, and they often got together after one of their sessions."

"So, you think maybe they still go there?"

"It's a possibility. But even if they do, how would you know when they would be there, or who was in the group for that matter?"

Gessie admitted Vanda had a point, and she let the matter drop. Vanda gave her a look like she didn't quite believe she was letting it go, but she didn't say anything. Instead, she poured each of them another glass of wine and looked kind of sheepishly at Gessie.

"Sooooooo," Vanda stretched out the word. "What do you think of Spence?"

Vanda had asked the question as she brought the glass of wine to her lips, partially obscuring her face.

"Hey, you don't fool me any more than I fool you," Gessie laughed. "I saw you were practically drooling when we were at Hattie B's, and it wasn't from the Hot Chicken. I think the word you used when you were giving me a hard time about Cole was "smitten." So, right back at you. It's obvious you are smitten with Spence. I only know what I read about him on the band's website, but he seemed like a great guy, and I think he's smitten with you as well?"

"You think so?" asked Vanda, beaming at Gessie's observation.

"Oh, please. You exchanged numbers, right?"

Vanda nodded but frowned a bit when she said he hadn't called her yet.

"He's probably like Cole and is upset about Gary. It sounded to me like Spence was just as determined to find out what happened with Gary as Cole was. Plus, Spence has the added stress of having to be a go-between for Cole because Gary's family doesn't want to talk with Cole and doesn't want Cole at Gary's funeral. That reminds me, I wanted to see if the obituary had been posted online yet. It would probably have the details for when the services will be."

Gessie jumped up from her seat at the counter, went over to her desk and booted up her laptop. Vanda stood behind her and watched over her shoulder as she brought up the Nashville newspaper and opened up their obituary section. Sure enough, there was a listing for Gary, and it said the funeral would be held the upcoming Monday. There was a brief bio for Gary, and although the cause of death was not mentioned, there was a request that in lieu of flowers, donations could be made to a local outreach program for drug rehab.

After reading the obit, Vanda thought she probably wouldn't hear from Spence until after that, and she certainly wasn't going to be the first one to call. Gessie agreed with Vanda and didn't think Cole would call her before that either. But what she didn't tell Vanda was that she couldn't stand the thought of Cole grieving alone. Unless something happened to change the Armbrusters' minds, Cole wouldn't be able to attend the funeral. She knew that was hitting him hard, and she wanted to be there for him if he needed company. That was why she had gotten the peaches. Gessie planned on baking the pie and taking it over to Cole. That's what people did. They took comfort food.

Vanda was looking at her funny, and Gessie knew she must have missed something Vanda had said while she was lost in thought.

"Since you obviously didn't hear a word I just said, let me repeat it," Vanda huffed. "Don't go and do anything stupid, especially by yourself. Call me, and I'll go with you."

Although Gessie assured Vanda she didn't plan to do anything stupid; she wasn't sure her friend believed her. Gessie didn't know how she did it, but Vanda seemed to read her pretty well. With her fingers crossed behind her back, Gessie told Vanda she was going to spend a quiet Sunday catching up on domestic chores and possibly working on a new song she had running through her head. She didn't feel too bad since baking a pie was domestic, and she did have a new song running through her head. So, she hadn't exactly lied. She just hadn't mentioned that she might go stake out the coffee shop Vanda had mentioned. It was a long shot, but she figured she could take her laptop with her to pass the time.

After Vanda left, Gessie did a quick search of the web pages for the churches downtown. She made a note of the times they had Sunday services. Gessie thought it was unlikely any NA or AA meetings would be held at the same time as those services. From what she learned, she decided she would plan to hit the coffee shop in the late afternoon. The worst that could happen was she wouldn't see anyone who looked like they had come from a meeting. But she knew for a fact that the coffee was good, and they also had some awesome pastries. So, there was no downside.

She had a little trouble getting to sleep because her mind kept running through scenarios about what she would say if she encountered someone from the NA group. She also wondered how Cole was doing, and that led her to working through some possible lyrics for the melody that had been running through her head. With thoughts of old friends and the way they touched your life, Gessie finally drifted off to sleep.

The next morning, Gessie was up at the crack of dawn and went out for a run along the riverfront. She kept an eye out for Cole but didn't see him. She was a little disappointed she hadn't heard from him but then scolded herself for being so self-centered. He had a lot on his mind, besides she hoped to have some new information before she talked to him next.

When she was back in her apartment, Gessie took a quick shower, made herself some coffee and toast, and then set about making the peach pie. She pulled out a beat-up looking Betty Crocker Cookbook her mother had given her when she first moved to California. It had been her grandmother's, and just flipping through it was a joy. The well-worn pages and a few stains here and there gave a hint to favorite recipes. Gessie opened the book to the pie section and did a quick scan of the recipes for making the pie dough and filling. Although it had been a while since she had baked, the steps came back to her quickly.

First, she mixed flour and salt, cut in the shortening, and sprinkled in some cold water until the pastry was the consistency she wanted. She formed a ball and then cut it into two portions, one slightly larger than the other. After rolling out both balls of dough, she let them both rest while she opened the brown bag and inspected the peaches. Gessie was pleased the fruit seemed perfect for the pie and quickly went about peeling, slicing, and then mixing them in a bowl with sugar, flour, cinnamon, and salt.

She draped the larger portion of the pastry dough into her ceramic pie plate, almost hating to cover up the design on the dish. It always made her smile. Her parents had given it to her one Christmas, and it had the Pi symbol stamped in the center of the dish, with the infinite numbers for Pi ringing the edge of the dish until running out of room. It was the perfect gift for the computer geek she had been at the time. And while she wasn't using her computer skills much at present, she could still appreciate the humor.

Gessie didn't usually use the special pan for pies she would give as a gift; she was always too afraid she wouldn't get it back. In this case, however, she didn't think that would be a problem, and it would mean she'd probably see Cole sooner rather than later because he wouldn't put off returning the dish.

She was humming "Me and Bobby McGee" as she put the filling mixture atop the pastry crust in the pie dish and then cut up some small cubes of butter that she sprinkled over the peach mixture. She placed the other portion of the rolled-out dough over the pie filling and began to pinch the upper and lower crusts together, so they formed a scalloped edge. After cutting several slits into the top of the crust, she grabbed some foil and fashioned two-inch strips around the scalloped edge as a cover so that it wouldn't get too brown as it baked. Now, all it needed was a little sugar on the top, and it would be ready to go into the oven.

Gessie was reaching for her sugar canister when she had another thought. Vanda used Sugar in the Raw for her coffee, and Gessie thought the golden, courser granulation of the raw sugar might give the pie a fun and interesting texture. She set the oven to preheat to 425 degrees, and then she picked up her phone off the counter and sent a text to Vanda asking if she could borrow a couple of sugar packets.

"Sure, come and get 'em," Vanda texted back.

Gessie had a big smile on her face as she opened the door. It was quickly replaced by a look of shock when she saw the man standing in the doorway, with his hand raised to knock on the door. It was too bad the Armani suit and perfectly styled hair couldn't make up for the arrogance and ugliness that radiated from him.

"Burton, what are you doing here?" Gessie asked in surprise.

Burton didn't say anything. He was too busy looking at Gessie.

Gessie saw the look of distaste on Burton's face as he took in her bare feet, yoga pants, and long black tee that was liberally sprinkled with bits of flour. Gessie had been having a good time baking for the first time in a long time. She hadn't cared if the flour got on her shirt, and wouldn't have been surprised if there were some on her face as well. She hadn't even bothered with any makeup after her shower.

"Burton," Gessie said more firmly, "what are you doing here?"

"I came to see if you had come to your senses and were ready to come home."

Gessie couldn't believe what she was hearing, but she didn't get a chance to respond because Vanda appeared beside Burton and looked at Gessie.

"Is this guy bothering you, Gessie?"

The look of distaste on Burton's face when he had first seen Gessie was nothing compared to his reaction at seeing Vanda. Although Vanda was beautiful, there was no way that fact would register with him. He was practically apoplectic as he took in Vanda's purple hair, piercings, and tattoos.

"It's none of your business, freak show. This is between Gessie and me."

As he said that, he sidestepped in front of Vanda and then barreled his way into Gessie's apartment. "Get inside," he commanded as he shoved Gessie backward from the doorway.

The push had surprised Gessie, and she tumbled backward and landed hard on her butt.

Gessie was a little dazed, but heard Burton growl, "Get up."

That was followed by another voice that said, "Don't lay another hand on her."

Gessie got another surprise as she raised herself gingerly from the floor. Detective Warner was behind Burton. He grabbed Burton's arms and was placing him in handcuffs.

Burton was in a rage. He was struggling against the hold Detective Warner had on him and was practically screaming. "What the hell are you doing? Who are you? Is this some kind of joke?"

Detective Warner spoke in a controlled and firm voice. "What I'm doing at the moment is detaining you. As to who

I am, that would be Detective Warner with the Metropolitan Nashville Police Department. I just witnessed you assaulting this young woman. I assure you I don't consider that a joke. Now, unless you want to continue being an ass and add resisting to possible charges, I suggest you calm down until I get an idea of what's going on here."

"What's going on here is that I've come to knock some sense into this woman and take her home."

"Poor choice of words and ones that don't give me much inclination to change my initial impression of you."

With that, Detective Warner looked at Gessie, "You want to tell me what happened, Miss Chapel?"

"There's not a lot to say, Detective. I opened the door and Burton--his name is Burton Halstead--was standing there. I haven't seen or talked with him in over a month. Unfortunately, I lived with him for a while out in California until I came to my senses and saw him for the egotistical, controlling person he is."

"Why you..." Burton started, but Detective Warner jerked him a bit.

"I'm not talking to you, Mr. Halstead. Keep quiet. You have anything to add?" Detective Warner asked Vanda.

Gessie had been so focused on what was happening with Burton and the detective; she hadn't noticed Vanda had stepped inside the apartment as well.

"Not really. Contrary to what ol' Burton here said, my name is not Freak Show. I'm Vanda Dalton, and I was expecting Gessie over at my place. When she didn't show up, I looked out the door and saw this guy over at Gessie's. It didn't look like Gessie was happy to see him. So, I had just come over to see if she needed any help. That's when he got really ugly, and then he shoved Gessie. Of course, you had shown up at Gessie's door about then and saw that part for yourself."

Detective Warner nodded at Vanda and then looked back at Gessie. "I'm assuming you do not want this man on your property."

"That's correct. What's going to happen with him?"

"Well, from everything I've heard and seen, I'm classifying this as a case of domestic violence. Under Tennessee law, the arresting officer has some discretion as to what charges will be made."

For some reason, that brought out a smug smirk on Burton's face. He must have thought Detective Warner was just going to give him a slap on the wrist and a knowing wink. So, he was totally shocked when Detective Warner continued.

"The preference under the law is for arrest, and that is my preference as well. What will happen, Miss Chapel, is I'm going to call an officer who will take Mr. Halstead here downtown and book him on a domestic violence misdemeanor. Unless he's got some pull here in Tennessee, I'm pretty sure he'll spend at least a night in jail before he can appear before the judge. If this is his first offense, he'll probably be issued a fine and then released."

Detective Warner said he still wanted to talk with Gessie after he had handed Burton off to another officer. Burton didn't go quietly. He was calling Gessie every name in the book and insinuated that she and Detective Warner were in some sort of lurid affair. Detective Warner must have said something to Burton at that point because there were no more shouts as they made their way through the courtyard.

CHAPTER 15

As soon as the door shut behind the Detective and Burton, Gessie began to shake. Vanda walked over and hugged her.

"Are you okay? Why don't you sit down? I'll get you some water."

Gessie didn't say anything; she just did as Vanda had told her to do and sat down in one of the dining chairs.

"Ooooh, Vanda said when she'd reached the kitchen. A pie! I bet that's what you needed the sugar for."

"The pie!" Gessie cried, snapping out of her daze.

Gessie jumped up and joined Vanda in the kitchen. "I've got to get this into the oven. I hope sitting out like this didn't ruin it somehow."

"I think you should take this water and sit down. I can finish the pie."

"No, no. I'm fine. I'm making it to give to Cole. I thought he could use some comfort food. It'll just take me a minute, and then I will take that water."

Vanda reached into the pocket of her jeans and pulled out several packets of sugar, which she shook as she offered them to Gessie. "Still want these? I don't think being in my pocket for a few minutes is going to hurt anything."

"Thanks," smiled Gessie taking the packages. "I think a couple will do it."

Gessie got a small brush out of her utility drawer and then held it under the tap water for a minute. She brushed the water over the top crust and then opened a couple of raw sugar packets and sprinkled them over the crust as well.

She quickly put the pie into the oven and set the timer for 45 minutes.

"Okay, I'll take that water now. Grab one for yourself, and let's sit down. By the way, I apologize for Burton calling you a freak show. He is such a jerk. I still don't know how I didn't see that right from the first."

"There's nothing to apologize for. You know that stuff doesn't bother me. If I didn't want a reaction, I wouldn't call attention to myself. It's a good barometer. I can quickly measure people. And jerk is maybe the kindest word I'd use for Burton. How do you think he found you, and did he seriously think you were going to go back with him to California?"

"Knowing Burton, he probably hired somebody to do a skip trace or something. Burton probably could do one himself, but he wouldn't even think of it. Why do something yourself when you can just pay someone to do it for you. As for him thinking I'd go back with him. Yes, I'm sure he did think that. It would have been a shock to his ego that I left him. He can't imagine how I could have left him in the first place, and I'm sure he waited until he thought I had sufficient time to realize what a mistake I'd made. He was certain I'd jump at the chance to have him and my old life back. Before me, he had played the field. He was very charming initially. I didn't see the obsessive side of him until I had moved in with him. He became more and more possessive and verbally abusive. I was supposed to be grateful he chose me and that he was willing to bring me up to his standards."

"Wow. Just wow. Do you think he'll leave you alone now?"

"I have no idea. I didn't expect him to do this. It's more effort than I thought he'd make, even if his pride was seriously bruised," Gessie sighed.

There was a knock on the door, and Gessie looked through the peephole to see Detective Warner standing there.

"Come in, Detective," Gessie said as she opened the door. "Have a seat at the table there. I was just thinking about making some coffee. Would you like a cup?"

"I have to admit. I could use a cup right now. Just black is fine. And it's Dax."

"Dax?"

"My name," the detective said as he smiled at Gessie.

145

"Oh, of course, and feel free to call me Gessie."

Since no one seemed to be paying her a bit of attention, Vanda piped up. "Yes, I'd love some coffee, too. Just a couple of packets of Sugar in the Raw if you happen to have them."

Gessie looked over at her friend and laughed. She was still giggling as she busied herself in the kitchen, making three cups of coffee.

"Just an inside joke, Dax," Vanda said emphasizing the detective's first name, since he hadn't even looked over to include her when he'd given that bit of info to Gessie. "That's why I was on my way to Gessie's door. Gessie's making a pie and wanted to borrow some sugar. I just live across the courtyard."

Detective Warner nodded at Vanda almost absentmindedly because he had been watching Gessie the whole time Vanda had been speaking. He gave Gessie a big smile when she returned and set a mug of coffee in front of him. Along with Vanda's mug, Gessie made a little production of setting down a spoon and the two remaining packets of sugar she hadn't used on the pie. She went back to the kitchen, got her own mug of coffee, and then sat down at the table.

"I've got some follow up questions about the murder the other day. But before we get to that, let's talk about what just happened here. Would you rather talk in private?"

"Oh no, I'd just tell Vanda everything anyway, and she already knows most of it."

"Okay. So, about Mr. Halstead. That guy's a piece of work. People always think it's only dirtbags who abuse women. But those of us in law enforcement know better. A guy in a fancy suit with a high-priced job can be an abuser as well. Nothing came back on him from California, but I've seen guys like him before. Sometimes they just snap, and it looks like that's what has happened to Mr. Halstead. The humiliation of being arrested, topped with your refusal to do what he wanted, has caused an escalation in his actions. Am I correct that this was the first time he had been physical?"

Gessie nodded. "It was mostly verbal abuse before. We had a big argument the day I left, and I thought he was going to hit me. He didn't, but it made me see everything clearly. I wasn't going to wait around to give him another opportunity."

"Smart woman. There are too many women who aren't. The immediate problem, as I see it, is we can't be sure what effect his incarceration will have on him. I've given him a warning of what the penalties would be for a second violation, but I don't know if that will keep him from coming back here. You know him better. If you think he will stick around, I'd advise you to get a protection order."

"To be honest, Dax, I'm not sure if he'll come back or not. He's good at rationalizing things and can work up quite a story to justify his actions. He could convince himself he did all he could for me, but I was a lost cause. That way, he could go back to California, satisfied he had done everything he could to elevate me to his pinnacle of class. Or he could persist in believing I belong to him and will stop at nothing to take me back with him. I guess we won't know until we see if he shows up again or not."

"Unfortunately, there's not much we can do unless he does."

"Don't worry. Today surprised me. I'll be more prepared and aware now. I will get the protection order if he stays around here. And thank you for being here, Dax."

"I was just doing my job. Speaking of which, let's get to the other matter, and I can get out of your hair."

Gessie sat up a little straighter in her chair and did her best to keep her face expressionless when the detective asked her what she had been doing at Buddy Norman's Autoplex.

"I'm looking for a new car," Gessie stated.

"That Audi looked brand new. Is there something wrong with it?" The detective said the words in a matter of fact tone, but Gessie didn't miss the fact that he was watching her intently.

"How did you...Oh, were you there?" Gessie asked as sweetly and innocently as she could. She saw no reason to admit she had noticed the detective at the dealership. "I didn't see you. Anyway, to answer your question, yes, there is something wrong with the Audi. I don't drive much here. It's too big for my parking space, and I'm sure you'll understand this last reason. Burton insisted I buy it."

It looked like Detective Warner was going to challenge her a bit, but her last words caused him to visibly relax his posture, and his expression softened.

"Okay. I can understand that. But why that dealership? Do you know Buddy Norman? According to what you told me before, you didn't know Cole Trammel all that well. Were you aware Cole and Buddy had a history?"

"No, I'd never met Buddy Norman before. I knew of him. Anyone with a TV has seen his commercials, I'm sure. I happened to be watching my TV when one of those commercials was on. It seemed like an omen, and I just hopped in my car and drove out there. It was very spur of the moment."

This time Dax let her know she wasn't fooling him for a minute. "You left out the 'Well, fiddle-dee-dee' at the start of all that."

"I don't know what you mean," Gessie countered. But it took everything in her power not to affect a Southern accent at Dax's veiled accusation that she was putting on an act of innocence worthy of Scarlett O'Hara.

Dax raised an eyebrow, and his voice had a more serious tone as he continued. "Right. I'm sure some of that is true. So, I'll buy it, but you didn't answer my last question. Were you aware Cole and Buddy had a history?"

Gessie gave a little sigh. Dax's piercing blue eyes were looking at her very intently. But the look wasn't intimidating. It was more like he was searching within her, willing her to be truthful with him—to trust him. She realized she did trust him and wouldn't ever want the look to turn hard. Besides, she didn't have anything to hide. She lifted her chin slightly and met his intense gaze with one of her own.

"I wasn't aware of their history until I did some snooping on the internet. After we left you Friday morning, I invited Cole over here for some coffee. Anyone could see he was distraught, and he needed someone to talk to. He talked about how he knew Gary, and he mentioned Buddy Norman as well since they had all gone to high school together. He didn't get into much more than that because you called right about then advising him you wanted him to come into the station. So, you interrupted his story. I confess; I was curious. After Cole left, I wanted to know more about him. A search led me to the band's website, but it also led me to several articles about a lawsuit where Buddy Norman was often quoted."

"You didn't know about the lawsuit before."

"No."

"But you found out more later?"

"Look, Dax, I did talk to Cole again yesterday, and he volunteered information about the lawsuit. I'm sure you already have the same information, and I'm not going to talk about it. What I will say is that in the few times I have spoken to Cole Trammel, it is clear he loved Gary Armbruster like a brother. His death is tearing him up. If you think Cole had anything to do with it, then you are wasting your time while a killer is getting away scot-free. Now, I've got a pie I need to check on."

Dax looked at her for a moment longer, then he gave a wry smile and stood up. "I sure don't want to be responsible for burning that pie. It smells mighty good. You already have my card. Please call me if there's anything else you think I should know." When he reached the door, he turned and added, "And, Gessie, it seems you're snooping in more places than just the internet. Leave the detecting to the professionals. I can assure you we're pursuing several different areas in our investigation. The one thing you do need to watch for is that ex of yours. Take care, Gessie. Miss Dalton, you keep an eye out, too. Good-bye, ladies."

The timer on the oven dinged just as the door closed behind the detective. Gessie jumped up from her chair and went into the kitchen. She grabbed a couple of oven mitts and reached into the oven to pull out the pie. She set the pie on top of the range and took in the aroma.

Vanda had followed her into the kitchen and watched as Gessie gently pulled the foil from around the edge of the crust. "My goodness, that looks and smells wonderful. I can't believe I'm not going to get any of it."

Gessie laughed. It was good to have this nice distraction after the discussion with the detective. It kept her from fussing over every nuance of what was and wasn't said during their conversation.

151

"I promise I'll get some more peaches, and I'll make one for you, too."

"I won't let you forget. I think Detective Warner--that would be Dax to you--likes you."

"Whoa, Vanda, that came out of left field. What do you mean he likes me? He was very professional. I'm sure he was just trying to put me at ease. Besides, he's got to be close to 40."

"I don't think he's hit 40. But even if he has, so what? He's not dead. He's a good-looking guy, and it looks like he keeps in shape. I didn't see a ring, and I think he cut you a whole lot of slack he wouldn't have given to someone else. He didn't take his eyes off you."

"You're nuts. Of course, he kept his eyes on me. He was trying to catch me in a lie. That's what detectives do. What you thought you saw was probably just him feeling sorry for me after the whole Burton deal."

"Yeah, sure, that was it. Because homicide detectives are so touchy-feely. I'm going to leave you to your fantasy and remove myself from the temptation of stealing a slice of that pie. I've got a presentation I need to finish for a meeting tomorrow with one of my clients. Try to stay out of trouble."

Gessie thought about what Vanda had said about the detective. He did have the most incredible blue eyes that seemed to lighten or darken, depending on the man's intensity level. And some very faint lines that crinkled at the side of those eyes when he softened his gaze or when he smiled. She wondered what would happen when he actually laughed. She could almost imagine his face lighting up and his blue eyes dancing.

Whoa! What the heck was wrong with her. She was not interested in the detective. She'd barely admitted the feelings she was having for Cole. It had to be an overreaction to the whole Burton thing. First, Cole had come to her rescue, and now so had Detective Warner. She hoped she wasn't guilty of succumbing to some Damsel in Distress Syndrome, if there was such a thing. No, she'd give herself more credit than that. Plus, she had no desire to jump right into another relationship. She didn't want to be a cliché and find herself in a rebound relationship. Everyone always said those rarely worked out.

It wasn't going to stop her from helping Cole, however. She was still going to go through with what she had planned. She left the pie to cool and went up the steps to her loft to change.

CHAPTER 16

Since it was Sunday, Gessie decided she'd go a step up from her regular jeans and t-shirt. She put on a pair of gray pencil pants and paired it with a black crepe cap sleeve blouse. She took a little more time with her makeup too and went with some brighter shades so that the black top wouldn't wash her out. She formed her hair into a chignon and then gave herself a quick look in the mirror. She wanted to look professional but without an edge. She thought the look would go well with the image she wanted to project as she worked on her laptop at the coffee shop and yet not make her seem unapproachable.

She slipped her feet into a pair of black mules and then grabbed her laptop case. She slid the machine inside and filled the pockets with her billfold, keys, mace, and a flashlight. She was hoping not to be out after the sun had set, but thought she should make sure she had the flashlight just in case. The downtown streets were mostly well lit, but there were dark spots. At least she didn't have to worry about Burton showing up unexpectedly, since he was probably spending the night in jail.

Gessie knew she shouldn't find glee in that thought. But she couldn't help it. Mr. Perfect. In jail. She could just imagine how he must be taking it. Not well, that's for sure. For one thing, she knew he hated orange. Now that brought out a laugh she didn't even try to suppress.

Looking down at her watch, Gessie saw that she needed to get a move on if she wanted to try and meet up with Gloves before going to the coffee shop. Like her, Gloves didn't normally busk on Sundays, and while it wasn't a sure thing, it was possible he would go to the praline shop since it was a day off. If he did go, he would likely stick to his usual time and show up there about 3 p.m. If she left now it would give her plenty of time to chat with Gloves to see if he had found out any information for her and she could still make it to the coffee shop by four as she had planned.

The last thing she did before heading out the door was to cover the pie. It should be just perfect the next morning when she intended to give it to Cole.

When Gessie turned into Butler's Run, she saw Gloves sitting at one of the tables outside the praline shop.

"Hi, Gloves. I was hoping I'd find you here."

"Gessie! Don't you look so pretty," Gloves said initially, then his eyes flitted back and forth, and he added, "But something's wrong. Something happened. Are you okay?"

Gessie didn't know what had tipped Gloves off. She didn't know how he did it, but he was a keen observer of people. Maybe she was walking slower, or maybe he had noticed she was a bit more wary. It had dawned on her as she walked down 2nd Avenue that it was just possible Burton did know someone with pull in Nashville, and he might not be in jail after all.

Gloves jumped up and motioned for her to sit down while he went inside the shop and brought her out a bottle of water and a pecan praline and then insisted she tell him what was wrong. He sat reasonably still for him as he listened to her describe the scene with Burton.

"Do you have a picture of this guy?" Gloves asked.

Gessie pulled her phone out of one of the pockets in the computer bag. She didn't use the camera feature on her phone often and so didn't access the photo gallery often either. Because of that, she had never even thought about the fact she had pictures of Burton there. If she had thought of it, she would have deleted them. She now found one that had a close up of Burton and showed the picture to Gloves.

"Send that picture to me, Gessie? I'll share it with the buskers. Other folks, too. Folks can be watching for him. Won't let trouble come for you."

Gessie started to say she didn't think that would be necessary, but then she hadn't thought Burton would show up in the first place. So, she decided it wouldn't hurt to have extra eyes. She sent the picture, thanked Gloves, and then eased into the real reason why she had sought him out.

"Soooooo," Gessie drew out the word. "Did you happen to find out any information about Gary Armbruster."

Gloves started fidgeting. It looked like he was bursting to talk but didn't want to talk about what she wanted to. Gessie just waited, and after a minute, the dam broke.

"Dangerous people, Gessie. Word is folks were trying to get him back as a customer. Nervous that Gary was staying clean. Going through the 12 steps. Watching him. Making sure one of his steps didn't include telling the cops about where he had gotten his drugs. Some friends not happy either. Gary didn't want to hang out with them anymore."

"Were there any names, Gloves?" Gessie asked.

"No names. Wouldn't tell you anyway. Dangerous people, Gessie."

Gloves frowned and fidgeted some more. Gessie knew there was something he wasn't telling her.

"Please, Gloves. What is it?"

After fidgeting a bit more, Gloves stood up and looked down at Gessie. "Some girl. No name. Not happy."

"A girlfriend?" Gessie asked. But Gloves wasn't saying anything else or didn't know. He patted Gessie on her shoulder and said he had to go.

"Be careful, Gessie. We'll be watchin' out for you. See you soon."

Gessie called out her thanks to Gloves's retreating back as he walked through Butler's Run toward the 1st Avenue exit. She thought about what Gloves had told her and then wondered if Dax was looking into Gary's previous drug connections and if he knew about any old friends who might have been unhappy Gary was clean--old friends other than Cole that is.

She surprised herself just a bit as she realized she had just thought of the detective as Dax. Vanda would have made something of it if she had known. She thought about calling him. Just to tell him about her conversation with Gloves, of course. But she stopped herself. She didn't think he'd be thrilled with her. He'd told her not to go snooping, and he'd barely gotten out the door before that was exactly what she'd done. She told herself she didn't know anything new anyway. Maybe she'd learn something at the coffee shop. Then maybe she'd call him. Maybe.

Gessie grabbed her computer bag and started walking up Commerce Street. She could tell the tourist season was over. What people there were out on the streets seemed to have a destination in mind. But it was a beautiful day for a stroll as far as Gessie was concerned. When she got to the coffee shop on the corner of 4th and Church, she stopped dead in her tracks. They were closed. She read the sign and saw the shop closed at Noon on Sundays. Now what? If that was the regular hangout for the NA members, where would they go if they still wanted to get together after a Sunday meeting?

She pulled out her phone and Googled coffee shops near her. There were several others, but the only one open at this time was Starbucks. It was open until 6:30 p.m. That was about the time it would get dark, and Gessie didn't plan to be there that long. The group would show up there, or they wouldn't. She might as well give it a shot for a while.

The Starbucks was just down the street, and Gessie decided even if she struck out today, a café mocha sounded good about now. She ordered a Grande and then did a quick survey of the room. A young man was sitting in a leather chair in one corner, tapping away on a laptop in front of him. An older couple occupied a small table near the windows. But that was it. When her café mocha was ready, she took it and sat at a small table that was positioned nearest to the largest table in the room. Gessie figured if a group did come in, they would likely sit at that table, and she might be able to pick up on any conversation.

Gessie opened her laptop and pulled up her music composition app. After plugging in her earbuds, she opened the file with the music for the latest song she had been working on. She was so engrossed in listening and then tweaking the notes, that it took a few minutes before it registered with her a group of people were standing at the counter.

She was surprised when she saw she had been there for 45 minutes. She almost hated to stop what she was doing; she had been making some progress with her song. But she reminded herself she had come here for a reason. She saved her file and took out her earbuds and then opened a book on her Kindle App so it wouldn't be too obvious she was doing nothing more than eavesdropping.

There were four men and two women in the group, and Gessie had been right. They got their drinks and then sat at the long table next to her. She didn't have to wait long to know whether this was a group from an NA meeting.

"To Gary," one of the men said to the others as he raised his coffee cup.

"To Gary," the others repeated as they all touched their cups together.

"I don't believe it," one of the women said. She lowered her voice a bit, but Gessie could still hear her next words. "Gary was so proud to get his one-month chip. He was doing good."

"Yeah, I thought so, too, Gloria. But you know how hard it is."

"Of course, I know how hard it is, Doug. That's why I get to see all of you so often." She gave a half-smile, and the group was silent for a few minutes.

"Maybe that girl got to him," one of the men finally said.

"What girl?" asked the woman who Gessie now knew was named Gloria.

"That's right; you weren't there that night."

The man who had spoken up told Gloria a woman had shown up at the last meeting Gary had been at the previous week. It was the first time any of them had seen the woman, and she didn't get up to speak. She had come in late and had sat in the back of the room. Gary had gotten up to speak and had faltered a bit when he saw her sitting there. It was obvious there was something he wanted to say, but he cut his talk short and walked immediately to the back of the room and spoke to the woman.

"He wasn't happy," said the other woman in the group. "I was in the back, too, and was just a couple of chairs over from the woman. He took the woman by the arm, and they went out into the hall."

"Did he say anything to her?" asked Gloria.

"He told her she shouldn't be there. And I'd say he was right. It was clear she was high. When they went out into the hall, I couldn't hear what Gary was saying, but he must have told her he didn't want to be around her. She was screaming at him that he'd never make anything of himself, and he'd be sorry. When he came back inside, he looked sad."

As the woman finished, she looked over at one of the men as if she expected him to pick up on the story. But the man just took a sip of his coffee and then asked the group if they were going to go to the funeral the next day. One of the men said he couldn't get off work, but all the others said they were going. That seemed to put an end to the conversation, and as they finished their drinks, they began to leave.

161

Eventually, there was only one man left, and he surprised Gessie by turning to her. "Did you hear everything you wanted?"

He hadn't sounded threatening, but he did make Gessie feel as if she was being reprimanded. She was sure her cheeks showed her embarrassment, but she looked the man right in the eye and held out her hand.

"I'm Gessie Chapel. You're right; I was listening. I knew Gary attended NA meetings around here and that a group often got together after the meetings for coffee. I was just taking a chance there'd be a meeting this afternoon and discovered this was the closest coffee place open."

The man seemed to consider Gessie for a moment and then shook the hand she was still holding out toward him.

"Frank Holden. You were a friend of Gary's?"

Before she answered, she asked Frank if he'd like another coffee, her treat. When he accepted, she ordered herself another café mocha and an Americano for Frank. While she waited for the drinks, she went back to her table, slipped her laptop back into the case, and then moved it to one of the chairs across the table from Frank. She walked back over to the counter just as the barista had finished preparing the two coffees, and she took them back over to the table, setting the Americano in front of Frank. She took the seat directly across from him and next to the seat where she had stashed her laptop.

Frank hadn't said a word during all this. Obviously, he had learned patience at some point in his life.

Gessie took a sip of her mocha and then decided just to be truthful.

"I didn't know Gary. But I happened to be there when my friend discovered his body."

"Ah, you know Cole Trammel," Frank said.

"Yes, I do. And the police seemed to be looking at him for Gary's murder. Cole loved Gary like a brother. He would never have done that. In fact, the police thought Gary had OD'd, and it was Cole who insisted there was no way that Gary would have OD'd like that, and someone had to have murdered him."

"I agree with you," Frank said simply.

"You do?"

"I do. Now, what brought you here? And who told you where to look? It's called Anonymous for a reason. Don't get me wrong; I'm not ashamed for you to know I was an addict. I've lived with it for a long time. I've also been clean for a long time. But it doesn't mean I don't get tempted now and then. This group helps, and while some of us are comfortable with the group and each other, there are others who need the anonymity. We don't normally talk about anything that happened in the meetings. Today was an exception. Everyone was upset when they heard about Gary. He hadn't been coming long, but everyone liked him."

Gessie took a moment to explain she only knew about the group in a roundabout way. She told him a friend of a friend had seen someone they knew having coffee with a group of people, and the person had ignored them. After the third time it had happened, the friend had finally admitted they were an addict and having coffee after some of the meetings and hadn't wanted to make anyone in the group uncomfortable with introductions.

"All I knew was it was a coffee shop downtown," admitted Gessie. "I Googled drug addiction programs and saw a couple of the churches in this area had a lot of involvement. I picked the one I thought was most likely and then looked for nearby coffee shops. I was just hoping there would be a meeting this afternoon, and this was the only coffee place open."

Frank seemed to think all that over. "What were you hoping to learn?"

"I was just hoping to learn more about Gary and maybe find out something that would help take the attention off Cole. He's just devastated, and he can't even go to the funeral. Gary's folks told him straight out that they didn't want him there. I don't know if they think Cole murdered him, but they certainly blame him for Gary becoming an addict in the first place. But from what Cole told me that wasn't the case. And Gary had called Cole just before he died. He wanted to mend fences with Cole."

Frank gave a wry smile at the mention of the phone call. "I'm glad to hear that."

CHAPTER 17

Gessie sensed Frank Holden had come to a decision of some sort. So, she took another sip of her café mocha and waited.

"I was Gary's sponsor. What you overheard earlier was right. Gary was doing good."

Frank explained that Gary's stint in rehab had been very successful, and he was committed to keeping clean. Most of the guys at the recovery center were good eggs, but he said Gary had called him a couple of times after one of the residents had approached him, pushing Gary's previous drug of choice. Frank had some contacts at the recovery center and made it known there was a problem with one of the residents. That guy had been kicked out of the house.

"So, that guy might have known Gary was somehow the reason he got kicked out? Would the guy have killed Gary for it?"

"I don't know," answered Frank, "Gary didn't mention seeing the guy after he got kicked out, but it was just two weeks ago."

"What about the woman who showed up to the meeting?"

"Yeah, Gary stuck around after the meeting that night to talk to me. It really upset him. He'd known the girl for a long time. Even though he felt something for her, they had also done drugs together. One of the things they stress in rehab is to avoid people who would get you back into the life. She came to the meeting saying she was giving up drugs so she could be with him. But like Wendy said, it's hard to believe someone is going to quit when they are so obviously stoned when they're saying it. I know he'd talked to the woman before. She was one of the people on his list to make amends with. In her case, it would have been a bittersweet apology since he would have also made it clear he wouldn't be able to be around her. She didn't take it well."

"Did he tell you the woman's name?"

"No, he didn't. We're pretty good around here at not mentioning names. I'm pretty sure some of the names we do know aren't real ones."

Frank gave that same wry smile, and it reminded Gessie she wanted to know what had caused the first one.

"Frank, you kind of smiled when I mentioned Gary had called Cole. Why is that?"

"We'd talked about it. Cole Trammel was the one person Gary wanted to make amends with and the one he was most afraid to get in touch with. He had an excuse for a while since Cole was out on tour. But Gary knew Cole was back in town, and he had been trying to get up the nerve to call him. I'm glad he did it before he died. I'd like to think it gave him a little peace."

"Well, I know Cole was thrilled. He told me Gary sounded like he used to and was beyond happy at the thought they could be friends again. Gary also told Cole he was going to drop the lawsuit."

"Yeah, Gary told me he was going to drop the lawsuit. He didn't tell me much about it, but he did say he was kind of fuzzy on the whole thing. He'd had a lot of time to think in rehab, and he wasn't sure what it said in the lawsuit was true. He said he'd kind of been talked into filing the lawsuit. He wanted to talk to Cole and get it straightened out. Most of all, he just wanted him and Cole to be friends again."

Frank stood up suddenly and said, "Look, it's late. I've got to go, and they want to close up."

Gessie was surprised when she looked outside and saw Frank was right. Twilight had set in. She'd need to hustle if she was going to make it home before it was full-on dark.

Frank seemed to notice her being slightly nervous when she looked outside. "Did you walk here?"

When Gessie nodded and told him she would be okay walking home, he wouldn't hear of it. He said his car was right in the garage next door, and he insisted he'd drive her home. Considering she still didn't know if Burton was in or out of jail, Gessie decided she would be better safe than sorry.

It was a short drive, but it did give Gessie a chance to let Frank know she was going to tell the detective on the case what he'd told her, especially about the phone call.

"Right now, Dax...I mean Detective Warner, says it's just Cole's word that Gary was going to drop the lawsuit. You can corroborate it."

Gessie heard a chuckle from Frank.

"How is ol' Dax. I didn't know he had the case. And I didn't know they were looking at Cole. If Dax is working this, he would have eventually rooted around until he found out Gary was going to NA meetings. He would have shown up at ours at some point. Sure, you tell Dax you talked with me, and he can give me a call. He knows where to find me."

Gessie didn't have time to ask him how he knew Dax because they had arrived in front of the door leading into her apartment's courtyard. She thanked him for talking with her and for the ride home. She noticed he watched until she went through the door to the courtyard before driving away.

She hurried into her apartment, set her computer bag on the table, and then dug into the pocket where her phone was stowed. The screen lit up, and she debated with herself whether or not she should call Dax.

It was not even seven o'clock, but it was a Sunday. Of course, he had been working earlier in the day. But would he still be working now? Gessie picked Dax's card up from the table where she had left it and punched in the mobile number listed. She thought that would be the best number considering he might be off duty. Gessie was so pumped up about what she had learned that she had forgotten the detective might not be too happy with the fact she had been snooping as he had called it. When that thought did occur to her, it was too late.

Dax answered the phone with concern in his voice. "Gessie? Is something wrong?"

"Oh, no," she assured him. "I hope I'm not bothering you. It's just…"

Gessie was stammering a bit. She hadn't thought about what she was going to say. She could almost hear a resigned sigh on the other end of the line.

"Let me guess. You've been snooping. Gessie, I told you. That's dangerous. You…"

Gessie didn't let him finish. She wasn't hesitant any longer. Now, she was irritated.

"Look, I learned some things. I'm pretty sure they are relevant to your case and that you don't know about them."

"Hey, I'm sorry, okay? It's been a long day. I was just leaving. Have you had dinner?"

His question caught her off guard. "Dinner? No. I just got home. I…"

Dax interrupted her. "I haven't either. I've been craving spaghetti all day. Why don't you meet me at that restaurant next door to you in about a half-hour? I'll treat you to dinner, and you can tell me what's so important I need to hear."

Gessie started to say no just on principle, but her stomach growled at that moment, and she had to admit spaghetti sounded good.

"Okay."

After hanging up the phone, Gessie decided what she had on was fine, but she wanted to freshen her makeup. As she did so, she began to talk to herself. "Is this a date? No, it's just so I can give him information. If it's not a date, why did he say it was his treat?"

She was still fretting a bit as she pulled her hair out of the chignon and decided to clip it up into a messy top knot. It was a little more feminine for dinner out, whether it was a date or not. She fussed with a couple of loose curls so that they framed her face, and after a last look in the mirror, she grabbed her Coach tote and went back downstairs where she transferred the things she needed out of her computer bag into the tote. She added her phone and then went out the door.

As soon as she stepped into the courtyard, she saw Dax leaning against the wall just inside the courtyard door. He pushed himself off the wall when he saw Gessie and walked toward her.

"I got here a little early. So, I thought I'd make sure there wasn't anyone else lurking in the courtyard waiting for you other than me."

The detective's eyes twinkled, just like Gessie thought they would when he smiled at her. She couldn't help but smile back.

"Thanks for watching out for me, Dax. Burton isn't out of jail, is he?"

"No, he's still there. From what I understand, he'll probably be on the docket to see a judge first thing in the morning. But you do seem to draw trouble around you. So, I thought I'd just make sure."

Gessie gave a little frown at that last comment. "I don't think that's true," she protested.

Dax didn't answer. He just raised one eyebrow and gave her a look that said, "Really?"

Gessie was about to protest again, but when she thought about her last few days, she had to wonder if Dax wasn't right. She'd had the incident with the drunks; she'd run right into a murder scene; and had her crazy ex-boyfriend show up.

She decided to let it go and walked with Dax out of the courtyard and on to 2nd Avenue. It was only a few steps to the restaurant, and they were quickly ushered to a table once inside. The restaurant was about half full, and they were seated at a table in the back of the room. Dax pulled out a chair for her, and once she was seated, he took the chair across from her.

"So, it's a real thing, I guess," said Gessie. When Dax gave her a quizzical look, she added, "The whole you've gotta sit with your back to the room."

Dax laughed. "Yeah, it's real. At least for every cop, deputy, and agent I know. Our eyes are usually on a constant survey of any room, although it's not always easy to do when you are distracted by your company. You look nice, Gessie."

Dax's tone had softened as he looked at her, and Gessie could feel herself blushing. The truth was she was attracted to Dax. But she was conflicted. After all, he was investigating Cole, and she was attracted to Cole, too.

"Thank you, Dax. Tell me, do you take all your suspects to dinner?"

"Only the pretty ones."

Dax was teasing her, but Gessie didn't get a chance to respond. The waiter came to take their order, and since they both already knew what they wanted, they gave him their full order. Gessie ordered a Chianti, and the baked lasagna and Dax ordered a beer and the spaghetti and meatballs.

Dax must have sensed he'd made Gessie a little uncomfortable if not a little irritated.

"You were never a suspect, Gessie," Dax said more seriously, "I just needed to clarify a few things from your original statement and see if there was anything you had forgotten. I wouldn't be doing my job if I didn't do that. I was hoping you'd stay out of things, but you obviously haven't."

Gessie didn't know whether to be amused, flattered, or irritated, and Dax wasn't helping. One minute he was teasing her; the next, he was straightforward, and then he went into lecture mode. The waiter chose that moment to bring their drinks, bread, and salads. Other than a tilt of his bottle of beer in an informal toast toward Gessie, the two of them didn't say anything while they tucked into their bread and salad.

After a few bites and a sip of his beer, Dax spoke up again. "That's a lot better. I was starving. I missed lunch. This, at least, takes the edge off. Look, I've got to admit I'm a little grumpy. This case is not an easy one. I'll take information any way I can get it. I just don't like the idea of you putting yourself in danger."

Gessie thought he sounded sincere, and maybe she had been a little on edge herself.

"You haven't seen me at my best, Dax. I'm not some victim. I can take care of myself, and it's not in my nature to sit back on the sidelines. If a friend is in trouble, I'm going to do my best to help them."

Dax was nodding. "I would like to get to know you better, Gessie. Maybe when this case is over, we can make that happen." He didn't wait for a response from Gessie. "But that's not why we're here tonight. There's something you want to tell me, and I do want to hear it. And now's your chance. Our entrees are headed this way, and I'll be all ears,

174

because my mouth is going to be very busy slurping down my spaghetti. Watch out for flying sauce," he added.

That made Gessie laugh. Spaghetti could be dangerous, no matter how careful you were. That's why she had ordered lasagna. Meeting or date, it didn't matter. It was never good to have sauce dripping down your chin and landing on your blouse. In between bites, Gessie began to tell Dax about what she'd learned.

"First, to put your mind at ease, I wasn't out on the street talking to drug dealers and such. A friend of mine asked around, and I'll just say that word on the street is that Gary was clean and wanted to stay that way although some people were trying to get him back into his old life. One of those people was an old girlfriend. There was also a man who was angry at Gary because he blamed him for getting him kicked out of the recovery residence. And most importantly, I have a source who can corroborate that Gary was planning to call Cole and let him know he was going to drop the lawsuit. Plus, there were witnesses to an argument Gary had with a woman, probably the old girlfriend."

As he had promised, Dax had listened and not interrupted. He'd made a good dent in the mound of spaghetti on his plate. Gessie waited, half expecting to get another lecture. But Dax surprised her again.

"That's some good info, Gessie. We talked to the people at the recovery residence, of course; they confirmed Gary was doing well. They didn't mention anything about a possible issue between Gary and one of the residents. Vice put out some feelers, and they are of the same opinion that Gary wasn't using. I've talked to several of Gary's old friends, including a woman who had made frequent calls to Gary. You said you had a source. You have a name?"

Dax wasn't pressing her, but that didn't mean he didn't expect her to give him a name. She was so glad Frank Holden had been willing to talk with Dax.

"Yes, I have a name. I guess you know the guy because he said you'd know how to find him."

Dax's expression showed he was intrigued. "Really? Who?"

"Frank Holden."

CHAPTER 18

At the mention of Frank Holden's name, Dax sat back in his chair. He seemed almost lost in thought for a moment, but the waiter chose that time to ask if they wanted any dessert, mentioning their tiramisu. Getting a nod from Gessie, Dax ordered a tiramisu for them to share, two coffees, a couple of to-go boxes and the check.

"Wow," Dax said as the waiter retreated. "Frank Holden. There's a name I haven't heard for a while. How do you know him?"

Gessie explained that she didn't know him. That led to her giving Dax the same rundown she had given Frank on how she had found the NA group at the Starbucks. Dax told her he was impressed with her luck over and above her deductive skills.

"Frank used to be on the job."

When Gessie gave him a quizzical look, Dax explained "on the job" meant he had been a cop. Dax and Frank had been in the police academy at the same time. Frank had been

177

assigned to Vice and was a decorated officer. But his wife was killed in an automobile accident, and Frank went off the rails for a while. Alcohol and drugs, the latter being easy for him to get since he knew more than a few dealers.

"I'm glad to hear Frank is doing well now. I do know how to find him. I'll check out what he has to say. And I'll take another pass by the recovery residence and with the girlfriend. I'll be honest with you, Gessie. I don't think your friend Cole did this, but I do have to continue investigating him, if only to rule him out. If the info you found pans out, it can help do that. I won't lie. This is good information. But can you please leave it to me now?"

"Will you let me know what you find?"

Dax told her he'd let her know what he could, but she had to remember it was an ongoing investigation. Gessie pursed her lips but didn't argue. She supposed he had a point. He had to do his job, and she knew he couldn't share a lot of what he did.

As the tiramisu and coffee arrived, Gessie took the conversation in a whole different direction. "What about you, Dax? Have you ever been married?"

Dax had just taken a sip of coffee, and he choked. Gessie started to get up to pat him on the back, but Dax held out his arm. "I'm okay," he managed to sputter as he reached for his glass of water.

Gessie narrowed her eyes. Vanda had been the one to point out the detective hadn't been wearing a ring. But some men didn't. Gessie steeled her expression and gave Dax a hard stare.

"No. No. I can see what you're thinking. I'm not married. You just caught me off guard. You continue to surprise me. One minute you're all serious and give the impression you want to keep me at a distance, and the next, you're asking me personal questions all innocent like."

"Like I said before, you haven't seen me at my best. You don't really know me."

"Well, I'm not sure about the former, and I'd like to rectify the latter. Full disclosure, I'm divorced. Have been for a couple of years now. That's another stereotype that's true. Being a cop and especially a homicide cop is not always good for a relationship. Come on; I'll walk you home."

Dax had paid the check, and Gessie noticed he left a nice tip. He stood up and came around to move her chair away as she stood up. He then placed a hand at the small of her back as he escorted her out of the restaurant. She was conscious of his touch, and it made her think of Cole. When Cole had touched her, there was an electricity. With Dax, it was different. She felt warm and safe and something else. Happy. She felt happy. Hmmm.

Neither of them spoke as they walked back toward her apartment. It had seemed natural to Gessie to slip her hand into the crook of Dax's arm as they walked back toward her apartment. They entered the courtyard and stopped when they reached Gessie's door. She reached inside her tote for her keys, and once she had them in hand, she turned to Dax, who was standing slightly behind her.

"Thank you for dinner, Dax, and thank you for taking both me and my information seriously."

"It was my pleasure, Gessie, and don't worry; I'll find out who was responsible for Gary's murder. When it's all over, can I call you, Gessie? I meant what I said. I'd like to get to know you."

Gessie wasn't sure what possessed her. "I think I'd like that." Then she quickly turned and put her key in the lock. She turned the knob and pushed the door open just a little. She was just about to go inside when she heard Dax mutter what sounded like, "Ah, hell."

Then he said her name softly. When she turned back toward him, he closed the space between them, took her into his arms and kissed her. The kiss started slow and then increased in intensity. This wasn't a spark of electricity; this was a full-fledged circuit overload.

When the kiss ended, Gessie was weak in the knees, and "Wow" was what she was thinking. Or maybe she had said it out loud. She wasn't sure. If the look on Dax's face was any indication, he had to be feeling the same thing she had.

Then a big grin crossed his face. "I'll see you soon, Gessie."

Gessie was still standing, dazed, in her doorway. "Wow," she said again. She changed her mind about going inside and instead locked the door back up and did an about-face, walking across the courtyard to Vanda's door.

When Vanda opened the door at Gessie's knock, the first words out of Gessie's mouth were, "He...he kissed me."

Vanda's eyes went wide, and she pulled Gessie into the apartment. "Who kissed you? Cole?"

Gessie was shaking her head, and she was absentmindedly touching her fingers to her lips.

"Not Cole," Vanda said mostly to herself as she took in Gessie's dazed state. Then it dawned on her who Gessie must have been talking about.

"You. Are. Kidding me. Detective, you can call me Dax, Warner? He kissed you? Just now? Come on, Gessie, snap out of it. This is epic. I need details. All the details. Sit. Wine or water?"

Gessie managed to pull herself together enough to tell Vanda she'd like some water, and by the time Vanda came back with a bottle from the refrigerator, Gessie was ready to talk.

"Start at the good part," Vanda grinned as she sat across from Gessie. "It must have been a doozie!"

Just the thought of the kiss again made Gessie's heart flutter. "I've never been kissed like that," Gessie finally said. "I'm so confused."

Over the next few minutes, Gessie filled Vanda in on everything she'd done since the whole ordeal with Burton that morning. As she retold the story of meeting with Gloves and then finding the NA group and Frank Holden, Vanda had worked up a pretty good scowl on her face.

"Hey, you weren't supposed to go out on your own. What if Burton had gotten out of jail. What if those NA people took exception to you ignoring their whole anonymity thing? You should have let me come with you."

"You were busy. Burton was in jail, and everyone was perfectly nice. Like I keep telling everyone, I can take care of myself."

"Okay, okay. Let's get back to the good stuff. So, this Frank guy dropped you off after you talked with him, you called Dax to tell him what you'd learned so he'd stop looking at Cole as a suspect, and his response was to invite you to dinner? I told you he liked you."

Vanda had said that last bit a bit smugly, and Gessie tried to act nonchalant, but she couldn't keep the smile from spreading across her face.

"Yeah, I'm pretty sure he likes me." Gessie blushed as she said it and then told Vanda that Dax had said he'd like to get to know her better but had to wait until after this case was over before he could do it.

"He said I wasn't a suspect, but since I was friends with someone who is..."

Vanda interrupted, "Speaking of that friend, what about him?"

"What do you mean?"

"You know exactly what I mean, Gessie Chapel. Yesterday, everything was about Cole. You were baking a pie for him this morning. Are you still planning to give it to him tomorrow?"

"Yes," Gessie responded immediately. "I can't bear to think of him all alone in his condo during Gary's funeral. Everyone else he knows will probably be at that funeral. I don't know what I feel for Cole. I know there's a connection there, but at this point, we're just friends, and I intend to be there for him."

"Okay, okay. Don't get mad at me. I'm here for you whether you end up with one, both, or neither of them."

"I can't think about it anymore. I wasn't looking for a relationship. I'm still not sure I'm looking for a relationship. Cole is hurting, and I think he's got enough going on, Dax could forget about me by the time this case is solved and another is likely to take its place, and goodness knows Burton is lurking in the background to remind me I don't want to jump into anything."

"I'm not sure who you are trying to convince. I'm not buying it, and I doubt you are either. Don't worry. You'll figure it all out. I'm just happy you're finally seeing what it feels like to have your toes curl when a guy kisses you. Now, go home and have sweet dreams. Some of us have to get up and go to work tomorrow."

Vanda walked Gessie to the door, gave her a quick hug, and told her she'd be available to talk again the next day after Gessie had seen Cole.

All of a sudden, Gessie was exhausted. The day had been a whirlwind of activities and emotions. She was practically a zombie as she walked up the stairs to her loft, changed out of her clothes into her favorite sleep shirt, and promptly flopped into bed. Vanda was right about one thing. She did have sweet dreams and a lingering sensation of Dax's lips against hers.

CHAPTER 19

Gessie woke up as the sunlight came streaming in through her loft window. She'd slept a little later than she normally did, but thought there was still time to get in a short run. She felt terrific after the run and a long shower. She put on a pair of skinny jeans and a silk tunic blouse and slipped her feet into her favorite pair of Vans. The ones with the Snoopy characters on them. She had decided she wanted to look anything but somber when she went to see Cole.

After putting on some mascara and a touch of blush, she went downstairs to fix some breakfast. She'd just finished a bowl of cereal and put her dish and spoon into the dishwasher when she heard her phone ringing. She hurried over to the table where she had set the phone after her run and was surprised when she saw Dax's name on the Caller ID.

He had said he wouldn't be calling her until after the case was solved. She didn't think he'd have had time to do that between now and dinner last night. So, she was afraid this call couldn't be a good thing. And she was right.

"Gessie, Burton is out."

"Oh."

"Gessie, the judge fined him and gave him a warning, but he didn't look contrite to me."

"You were there?"

"Yeah, I wanted to make sure I knew how the hearing went, and I wanted to let you know as soon as he was released. Gessie, I want you to be careful. I'm not sure he paid any attention to the judge's warning. I've got to go now, but you call me if he shows up anywhere around you. I'll be there. Nothing's more important to me than you being safe."

"Okay, thanks for letting me know, Dax," Gessie said softly.

"I mean it, Gessie. If you feel like you're in danger, call 911. Then call me. Even if you just get a weird feeling he's watching you, you call me." When Gessie didn't say anything, he spoke with a little more force. "Promise you won't take any chances, and you'll call."

"I promise. I'll be careful. And I'll call if I get a sense anything is wrong."

That seemed to satisfy Dax, and he hung up, saying he was on his way to the recovery residence to check out the information Gessie had given him the night before.

That made Gessie feel a little better, and she tried to put thoughts of Burton out of her mind. She put the pie into a carrying case made for that purpose and then did a check through her tote bag. She moved her canister of mace into a spot that could be quickly accessed and did the same with her phone. There was still an hour before the funeral was scheduled to start, but she thought by the time she got to Cole's place, he would already be out of his mind pacing back and forth in his condo.

She grabbed her tote and the pie and was out the door and halfway through the courtyard when she remembered she needed to be aware of her surroundings. Fortunately, Burton wasn't lurking in her courtyard, and she vowed to be much more watchful as she walked to Cole's house.

It was too early for most of the buskers to be out on the street, and while she could see some of the shop owners moving about inside their stores, most of them weren't open yet. Still, she exchanged a wave from a couple of the shop owners who looked out at her as she passed by. She didn't get any sort of strange feeling until she was juggling her tote and the pie case to open the door to the lobby for Cole's condo. The hairs on the back of her neck prickled and she glanced around nervously. She didn't see anyone and decided she was just paranoid. Once inside the building, she set her bag on a chair in the foyer and pulled her phone out of the tote's pocket.

"I'm in the lobby. Thought you might like some company. I come bearing pie," Gessie texted. When she didn't get an immediate reply, she thought for a minute she might have been wrong. Maybe she'd been too presumptuous. Maybe Cole wanted to be left alone.

But after a minute, her phone indicated she had a text, and she gave a sigh of relief. Cole had texted, "Come on up."

When she got to the eighth floor, Cole's door was open. Still, she knocked lightly and called out. "Peach pie, coming through."

"Hi, Gessie," Cole said as he came from the kitchen area and greeted her in the foyer. He gave her a hug. It was a bit awkward with her tote on her shoulder and the pie carrier in her hand. Still, it was nice, and even under the circumstances there was that tingle, spark, whatever you want to call it when the two of them were in close proximity.

"This is awful nice of you, Gessie," Cole said as he held out his hand for the pie carrying case. "Here, let me take that. Go on around and sit at the counter. I'll slice up this pie while the coffee finishes brewing. You are going to share it with me, aren't you?"

There wasn't a lot of inflection in Cole's voice, and Gessie could see he was hurting. He was trying to keep it together, though. She put on a smile and told him she was hoping he'd want to share. She went around and sat at the counter, watching him through the pass-through and babbling on a little about how she hadn't baked for a while, so she wasn't sure how good the pie would be. So, the least she could do was eat some too.

"Well, it looks terrific," Cole said as he removed the pie from the carrying case and set it on the kitchen counter. He cut two pieces and put them on plates he'd pulled out of one of the cabinets. He was about to pick up the plates when Gessie saw him look back at the pie plate. His back was to her so that she couldn't see his face. But his head sort of tilted to the side as he bent down a little for a closer look at the dish. Then he laughed. "Pi. It's a Pi plate."

"Yep," Gessie grinned, glad to see Cole laughing.

"You are something, Gessie Chapel," Cole said as he set a mug of coffee and a piece of the pie in front of her. That was quickly followed by a fork and a napkin--in the form of a paper towel--he had torn off a roll on the kitchen counter.

"This pie looks like it deserves fine china and linens, but you'll have to settle because I'm more interested in tasting it right now. My mouth is watering. Peach pie is my favorite."

As soon as the second cup of coffee finished brewing, Cole set his mug and his pie on the counter, grabbed his fork and napkin, and then hurried around to sit on the chair next to Gessie.

Gessie raised her fork but then pointed it toward Cole's piece of pie. "Go ahead. You first."

From the satisfying moans and the expression on Cole's face, it looked like he liked the pie. When he didn't say anything after a couple of bites, Gessie couldn't stand it.

"So? It's good?"

"You're interrupting my pie eating." There was a mock scowl on Cole's face as he tried to look like he was seriously irked that she was interrupting. But he couldn't hold it, and he laughed again.

"This is fantastic, Gessie. I'll deny I ever said it, but it's better than my mom's. I'm trying to figure out what the little bit of crunch is on the top crust."

Gessie was pleased and told him about using the Sugar in the Raw crystals for it.

Something in her expression must have changed because Cole put down his fork and looked over at her.

"Did something happen?"

"Uh..."

"You don't have to tell me if you don't want to."

"No, no. It's alright. I guess I'm not as good at compartmentalizing things as I'd like to be."

Cole didn't say anything, but he continued to look at her intently.

She started by telling him about Burton showing up at her door. Since she'd never talked to Cole about Burton before, she gave him the Cliffs Notes version of their relationship and how she had ended up in Nashville.

"I never thought he'd show up here. The situation sort of escalated, and he tried to push his way into my apartment, literally. Anyway, Vanda and Dax had shown up, and Burton was arrested."

Cole had been frowning during her story. "I'm glad someone was there before that jerk could hurt you any worse. I'll have to give Vanda a high five next time I see her. Who's Dax? Does he live in your apartment complex, too?"

Gessie hoped she wasn't blushing. "No. Dax. Detective Warner. He'd come by to ask me to clarify some information."

Cole's frown deepened. Gessie wasn't sure if he didn't like that she and the detective were on a first-name basis or just that he was most likely looking for more evidence against him. If it was the former, Cole didn't let on. But he did comment about the way Dax was investigating Gary's murder.

"I wish that guy would get it through his head that I had nothing to do with what happened to Gary."

Cole's good humor was gone, and he stood up, clearly agitated.

"I think he's coming around to that." Gessie had placed a hand on Cole's arm and motioned back to his chair. "Sit back down. I've got something else I wanted to tell you. This seems like the right time."

Gessie went through the same series of events and conversations she had already shared with Dax and Vanda. Cole didn't seem to be any happier about her investigating on her own than the others had. The difference was he didn't lecture her about it.

"I'm glad I didn't know what you were doing. I would have been worried about you," was all he said. "I wonder if that Frank Holden guy would talk to me. I'd like to talk with him about Gary. Hear how he was doing. I feel better knowing Gary thought of me as his friend again."

The mood was pretty melancholy after that. They finished their pie in silence, and Gessie got up to leave.

"I should probably go."

"I'm sorry, Gessie. I know I'm not very good company, but could you stay a little longer?" Cole had given a sideways glance to a clock in the kitchen. "Spence is going to come by after the funeral; could you stay until he gets here? You made me realize I'd rather not be alone right now."

"Sure. There's nowhere I have to be." Gessie remembered how Vanda had prompted both Cole and Spence to tell stories about Gary, and she asked Cole if he'd like to do that now.

"No. I don't think so. Spence and I have been doing a lot of reminiscing the last few days. What I'd like is if for you to sing something for me. One of your own songs."

Gessie didn't even think about protesting. The whole point was to make Cole feel better and take his mind off the fact that he wasn't at Gary's funeral. Besides, it would mean she'd get to play his awesome Gibson guitar. Gessie was trying to decide what to sing as she walked over and picked up the guitar. She looked around and then pulled out one of the chairs at the dining table. She liked to sit in a straight-backed chair with no arms to get in the way as she held the guitar in her lap.

She played a simple lead-in and started singing in a clear voice.

He caught me crying in our bed this morning,
Just as he was finally coming home.
I asked him where he was all last evening,
And why he didn't bother trying to call home

He told me that he'd spent the night a-thinkin.
Thinkin' about our love, but he had to go.
He told me that I was his everything.
He loved me but was leavin' to ride the rodeo

Broken once, broken twice, but still feeling,
A cowgirl's tears are flowing to the ground.
He looked at me and said he was a-leavin'.
A cowgirl's got a broken heart, when the rodeo's in town.

As Gessie got into the song, so did Cole. He had a big grin on his face and began slapping his knee in rhythm with the song. Gessie sang two more verses and when she ended on the last note of the chorus, Cole stood up and clapped.

"That was great Gessie. I'm curious where the idea for that came from."

Gessie laughed. "After I left California, I stayed in Kansas City with my folks a couple of weeks before I moved down here. My mother is an avid reader, and while I was there, I read one of the mystery novels she had in her bookshelf. It had a character in it that was in love with a professional bull rider. The song sort of just flowed out of my head and fingers. It was the first song I'd written in a long while, and as I was working on the melody, my mother would jump in with harmony. It has good memories for me. But I can sing something else if you'd like—something more recent. I've been working on my style."

"I would love to hear something else."

Gessie had to think for a minute. After successfully lightening the mood, she didn't want to sing anything that would ruin it. Gessie thought she might as well stick with "firsts" and decided to sing the first song she'd written after she'd arrived in Nashville. It was about someone staying true to themselves and knowing when they needed to walk away. She knew novelists were often advised to write what they know. It was no different for a songwriter. And she knew the feelings in the song very well since she'd lived through a situation that had caused those feelings.

It was a bit of a risk singing the song for Cole because she'd just gotten through telling him about her relationship with Burton. He was going to know it was based on that experience. She decided she was going to have to get used to people analyzing her songs, and her as well, if she was ever going to make a go of this whole singer/songwriter thing. She might as well go for it.

Cole had been waiting patiently for her to begin and she'd no sooner struck the first chord for the song's intro, when there was a knock on the door.

"Hold on," Cole said as he went to the door.

A moment later, he came back into the living room with Spence right behind him. Gessie figured she'd gotten a reprieve and had started to rise from the chair.

"Oh no, you don't, Gessie. Sit back down. You owe me a song. You're in for a treat, Spence. As a matter of fact, you're in for two treats. After Gessie sings a song for us, you get a piece of the peach pie Gessie brought over."

"Looks like I came at the right time then. Hi, Gessie. It's good to see you again."

Gessie couldn't help but smile as Spence took a seat on the couch and looked at her expectantly. He was a big man, but right now, he looked like he still had a lot of little boy in him. She wasn't sure if he was excited to hear her sing or because he wanted a piece of pie. Either way, Gessie started on the intro to her song once again. It was best to just get this over with and leave Spence and Cole to talk about Gary.

She didn't look up as she was singing. She was mostly concentrating on the chords and fingering. She was surprised to discover it was easier busking in front of people she didn't know than in front of someone she did. Vanda didn't count. She had been there from the start. But now, Gessie was nervous. Her voice caught in one spot, and she fumbled one of the chord transitions, and she was glad when the song was over.

It wasn't until then that she looked up, and she caught a look pass between Cole and Spence. She realized she wanted them to like the song and was anxious that neither of them had spoken. She looked back and forth at the two men. They were grinning, but she was starting to doubt herself when she noticed Spence give a nod to Cole, and he finally spoke up.

"That was great, Gessie."

"Really great," Spence agreed.

"It's just the kind of song we've been looking for. Would you be willing to come to our rehearsal Friday and sing the song for Matt and Trey? Especially for Matt. I think I told you he's the one who does all our arrangements."

Gessie could see Cole had finished speaking. His lips were no longer moving. But there was a buzzing in her ears, and she felt light-headed. The next thing she knew, Spence had taken the guitar out of her hands and Cole had gently pushed her head down toward her knees.

"Take a deep breath, Gessie."

The light-headedness seemed to pass and Gessie sat back up slowly. "I am so sorry. I don't think I've ever done that before. Of course, no one's ever told me they want to sing one of my songs before."

She was still in a bit of shock but was able to smile and take the bottle of water Spence was holding out to her.

CHAPTER 20

Gessie was on Cloud Nine when she left Cole's condo. She couldn't wait to get back to her apartment. She'd told Cole she'd be thrilled to come to their rehearsal on Friday but that she could send the band a copy of the song ahead of time. She could essentially generate the sheet music for the song using an app she had on her laptop. He'd asked if she had copyrighted the song, and she said that she had. It wasn't something she would have thought of doing on her own, at least not right away. But Vanda, being the business and marketing guru she was, had insisted that Gessie do that first thing as soon as she finished each song.

Cole had been glad to hear that because he said Matt had been cautious amidst the lawsuit hanging over the band to make sure they could properly attribute each song they performed. Mention of the lawsuit brought Gary to the forefront again, and Gessie had known it was time for her to leave. Spence had already been making a beeline for the pie as Gessie headed toward the door. Cole had walked her to the door and bent down to brush a kiss against her cheek.

When he'd thanked her for coming and told her again it had meant a lot to him, she had thought he was going to lean in for an actual kiss, but Spence broke the moment when he'd let out what could only be termed a guffaw. "It's a Pi plate!"

She might not have gotten a kiss, but she had left Cole laughing as she left.

"Mission accomplished," she thought to herself.

She had been so lost in thought; Gessie was surprised when she realized she was already at 2nd Avenue. She spotted Darla spinning her hula hoops up ahead and began reaching in her tote for a five-dollar bill as she crossed the intersection. She'd dropped the five into Darla's tip jar and gave her a smile and wave as she passed by. But she'd only gone a few steps when she heard Darla apologizing loudly to someone.

"I'm so sorry, sir. That one got away from me. Did I hurt you? Let me get that off you."

As each of the words had gotten louder, Gessie had turned to look at the commotion. Her eyes went wide. It was Burton. Darla had ensnared him in a hula hoop and was feigning a clumsy attempt at getting the hoop off him. What she was really doing was giving Gessie time to get away.

Gessie didn't waste any time. She sprinted for the courtyard door, and once inside, she did something the residents in her complex didn't usually do. She locked the courtyard door. Just like the gate leading out of the courtyard to 1st Avenue, the door on 2nd Avenue also had a lock. But the residents seldom locked that one. Vanda had told her the entry was so obscure they only had to worry about it when there was some big event going on at the Riverfront. They locked it then because people who did know about it, used it as a shortcut and sometimes thought the courtyard was an excellent place to party. The other residents might find it odd and somewhat inconvenient if the door was locked, but they all had keys.

Gessie hadn't been inside for more than a few seconds when she saw the doorknob turn. Then there was a pounding on the door.

"Open up, Gessie!" Burton shouted from the other side. "I'm not leaving."

There was more pounding, and Gessie thought she heard sirens.

"Go home, Burton," Gessie called through the door.

Gessie heard the sirens closer now, and Burton must have heard them, too, because the pounding stopped. She waited right where she was and could hear the siren chirping right outside the door. Gessie figured the police would probably talk first with whoever had called 911, but she knew they'd be knocking on the courtyard door shortly. She had no intention of opening it up until they did, however.

It dawned on her she had promised Dax she would call him if she saw Burton around. She fumbled for her phone and sent him a short text instead. "Saw Burton. Gone now. Police here."

She'd finished the last of the text when there was a knock on the door. Expecting to hear a police officer on the other side, Gessie was surprised to hear a familiar voice instead.

"Gessie, it's Darla. It's okay. He's gone. The police are here and want to talk with you."

Gessie threw open the door and immediately gave Darla a big hug. "Thank you so much. I owe you one."

"Well, you can thank Gloves, too. He made sure everyone knew what that guy looked like and told us we needed to be watching out for you. I gotta get back to my stuff," Darla said after giving Gessie a final hug.

The police officers told Gessie there wasn't much they could do since Gessie didn't have a protection order, which meant there was nothing to charge Burton with.

"He may have been scared away this time, but I suggest you get that protection order," one of the officers said.

Gessie heard another voice, "I agree. I can help her do that. I've got it from here, officers."

The two officers had blocked her view of the man speaking, but Gessie recognized the voice. As the two officers parted, she saw Dax. Her first reaction was to run into his arms. It would feel good right now to have him holding her. But she stopped herself. It probably wasn't a good idea since two men he worked with were standing right there. Besides, she'd been saying she could take care of herself. It wouldn't exactly look good if the first thing she did was look for a big strong man to protect her.

She tamped down her anxiety and waited as Dax finished talking with the two officers. Gessie was looking down at her phone as Dax walked toward her. There had been no return text from Dax. She tried to keep her voice even. "I didn't think you'd even seen my text. You got here fast."

Dax stopped no more than a foot away from her. He was studying her face intently. "I'm not sure you're as calm about all this as you'd like me to think, but I'm going to let it pass because you did contact me. I'd just left the Recovery Residence. So, I was nearby. I didn't want to stop to reply to your text when I could get here just as fast." Then Dax softened his tone, reached over and his hand brushed her cheek as he tucked a stray lock of hair behind her ear.

Gessie hadn't taken her eyes away from Dax, and she felt her heart racing. The moment seemed almost intimate, and her voice came out in a whisper. "Would you like to come in for coffee?"

Dax seemed to be warring with himself, but he took a step back and told her much as he would like to do that he needed to go.

"I followed that lead you gave me and have the name of the guy who blamed Gary for getting him kicked out of the residence. I'm on my way to interview him."

Gessie nodded. "Thank you for coming, Dax, and thanks for checking out what I told you."

"I told you I would. If you want to thank me, you can go online and pull down the form for an Order of Protection. I know a couple of judges pretty well, and I'll get you an appointment to make things easier. Probably later today or in the morning at the latest. You just have to fill out the form and file it with the court clerk. Then the judge can issue the order. It doesn't look like Burton is leaving town like we'd hoped."

Gessie assured Dax she'd fill out the form and that she wasn't planning on leaving her apartment for the rest of the day. Dax said he'd call her as soon as he'd gotten an appointment with one of the judges he knew, and then he watched as Gessie went into her apartment.

Once inside, Gessie set down her tote and flopped onto her couch. What a day, and it was barely half over. She was beyond angry with Burton. She should be enjoying the excitement she had felt when Cole and Spence said they wanted to record her song. It was just like Burton to spoil the moment. He'd been so good at that when she had lived with him. It was one of the many reasons she had walk away from the relationship. Yet here he was over a month and 2,000 miles later, still managing to cast a pall on everything.

Gessie decided it wasn't going to do any good to sit there feeling sorry for herself. So, she popped up off the couch, went over to the dining table, and opened her laptop. She'd

MURDER IN G MAJOR

get the whole form thing out of the way, and then she'd be able to concentrate on running the app to generate the sheet music for her song.

The form was pretty straightforward, and it only took her about 15 minutes to fill it out and send it to the printer she had over in one corner of the room. Gessie hated to have to go to such measures with Burton, but she must have pushed him over an edge of some sort. She hoped when they notified him of the order, he'd finally get it into his head that she wanted nothing to do with him, and he'd just go home.

She could hear the form printing out and tried to put it out of her mind. She pulled up her music app and gave it her full concentration. She wanted to make sure the song was the way she wanted it. It wasn't unusual for her or any artist, for that matter, to make little changes in the words or melody the more often they sang it. Just as she thought, the version she had recorded in the app had a couple of slight variations from the version she had just sung for Cole and Spence. She knew if Cole's band did end up recording her song, they'd likely make their own tweaks as well. And that was okay with Gessie. After making a few adjustments, Gessie sang the words to the music as it played out through her laptop's speakers.

Satisfied with the results, she generated the sheet music and emailed a copy of it to the address Cole had given her. The excitement she had felt earlier returned, and Gessie was feeling pretty good as she shut down her computer and went into the kitchen to make herself a sandwich. She hadn't had anything since sharing the piece of pie with Cole.

Thinking of Cole made her wonder if Dax was making any progress with the information she had uncovered. Dax had said he'd gotten a name from the recovery residence, and she wondered if he'd already gotten in touch with Frank Holden. She was pretty confident the old girlfriend who had shown up at the NA meeting was Rhonda Baxter, and she wondered if Dax would be talking with her again also.

After making herself a sandwich, she didn't even bother to go around and sit on one of the barstools. She just ate standing up in the kitchen. If nothing else, it made clean up a lot easier. As she munched on her sandwich, she was forming another plan. She wanted to get a better feel for Rhonda Baxter. It shouldn't be too difficult to dodge Buddy Norman at the Autoplex if she asked specifically for Rhonda. Besides, there was a Lexus SUV she had been taken with the other day. It was a compact model, had a full luxury package and all-wheel drive. She hadn't liked Buddy's smarmy sales pitch and innuendoes, but she did think he was right when he said she'd like to have the heated seats and steering wheel. The cold weather was something she hadn't had to deal with for several years.

The more she thought about the Lexus, the more she thought she should call Rhonda and ask for a test drive. She'd get a chance to see if she liked the car and pump Rhonda for information. But she couldn't do that until Dax called her and told her when her appointment would be at the courthouse.

Just in case the appointment was going to be later that day, Gessie decided that skinny jeans and Snoopy Vans might not be the right outfit for appearing before a judge. She should probably change into something more suitable.

CHAPTER 21

Dax had texted her just as she was about to go up to the loft. He'd asked if she could be ready in thirty minutes. When she responded that she could, she hurried up to her closet. She didn't have time to think about putting together a coordinated outfit. So, she just reached in and pulled out a cowl-necked sweater dress. It was a gray, long-sleeve dress that would be perfect for the day's cool weather, and she wouldn't have to worry about a coat.

She slipped the dress over her head, fussed with the cowl until it was draping the way she liked, and then quickly went into the bathroom to touch up her makeup. She decided to put her hair back in the chignon because she'd never liked her hair down when she was wearing something with a cowl-neck. She opened up the shoe box with her black Trotters low-heeled pumps and slipped the shoes on her feet. They were a soft leather and were cushioned inside. She'd seen the courthouse, of course, when she'd jogged through Public Square Park. There weren't that many steps leading up to the building. But she had no idea if they'd be taking stairs inside or if they would be standing around while they were waiting to meet the judge. She wanted to be comfortable.

Gessie had just gotten downstairs when her phone signaled a text. Dax said he was pulling up to the curb right outside the courtyard door. Gessie texted she'd be right out. She slipped her phone inside her tote and then went to the printer to get the pages of the form she had filled out.

She hurried out of her apartment and out the courtyard door. Dax was leaning up against a non-descript silver sedan. Non-descript except for the flashing bar of lights in the rear window. He stood up and reached down to open the car door for her.

Gessie liked the way he was looking at her. She knew the dress hugged her figure. It wasn't tight by any means. But it did look good on her. Maybe her selection of the dress hadn't been as random as she'd told herself when she was pulling it out of the closet.

"You look great, Gessie. Watch your head," Dax added as Gessie lowered herself into the car, put her knees together, and then rotated, gracefully pulling her legs into the car.

"Shouldn't I be in handcuffs and you pushing down on the top of my head, when you say that?" Gessie teased.

"What?" Dax shook his head as if to bring himself back into focus. He'd been looking appreciatively at Gessie's legs. "Somebody's been watching too much LivePD."

Dax hurried around the car and got into the driver's seat. He apologized to Gessie for not coming to the door to get her, but they were going to be cutting it close to make the meeting with the judge. The courthouse was so close they could have walked if they hadn't been in a hurry.

While they drove, Dax explained Gessie would give her form to the court clerk. Once it was entered into the system, the clerk would give it to a judge who would decide on whether or not to grant a temporary order or deny the petition until there was a full hearing. Dax had streamlined the whole process, and Gessie was ushered in to see a judge as soon as the clerk had finished processing her form.

Inside the judge's office, Dax introduced Gessie to Judge Grady, who was standing behind a beautiful cherrywood desk. She appeared to be somewhere in her 60's and was a tall, thin woman with an almost regal bearing. Gessie could imagine her with a stern face that would be very effective in the courtroom. However, she didn't see any of that at the moment. The judge was smiling warmly at Dax.

"I haven't seen you for a while, Dax. I guess you've been busy. Your mother said you were tied up on a case and had missed Sunday dinner."

Gessie didn't think the judge missed her look of surprise, nor the slight reddish tint that seemed to be coloring Dax's neck and moving up to his face. Sunday night had been when she had gone out to dinner with Dax. There was no way the judge could know that. Still, she seemed to give a smug grin, and her eyes were twinkling a bit as she settled into her leather chair and told Gessie and Dax to have a seat.

The judge looked at Gessie. "Okay, Miss Chapel, I have the paperwork in front of me, but I'd like to hear why you believe this Mr. Halstead would harm you."

Gessie gave the judge a brief description of her relationship with Burton and her decision to leave before it escalated to violence. She finished with how she had been completely blindsided when he had shown up in Nashville, and he had become physical.

"And you witnessed the physical contact, Dax?"

"Yes," Dax answered. Then he went on to describe how he had been coming to ask Gessie some follow-up questions for the case he was working and had arrived just as Burton physically assaulted her. He said everything matter of factly, as if he was giving testimony, but Gessie could have sworn the judge's lips twitched when Dax said he was just there to ask her some questions for his case.

"And you think immediate protection is in order, Dax?"

"Judge Grady, the arrest and night in jail seemed to have made no impression on the man. He appears to be stalking Gessie. From a couple of comments he made at the time of his arrest, I believe he intends to take Gessie back to California with him, forcibly, if necessary."

Gessie gave an involuntary shudder. She hadn't considered Burton would go so far as to abduct her.

"Okay, I'm issuing the temporary order. It will be effective immediately. The Sheriffs will go to his hotel and serve him with a copy of the order."

There was a knock on the door, and a clerk appeared telling the judge she was due in court. Everyone stood, and the judge came around the desk and extended a hand to Gessie. "It was very nice meeting you, Miss Chapel. I am sorry it was under these circumstances. But I can tell you are a smart lady, and you have taken the appropriate actions for this situation. Stay safe."

The judge then turned to Dax. "I'll see you at Thanksgiving."

The judge reached for her black robe, hanging on a hook in the corner of the room, and the three of them walked out of her office.

When they were back in Dax's car, Gessie was the first to speak. "So, I know you said you knew a couple of judges, but..." She let the sentence hang.

"Yeah, in hindsight, that might not have been my best move to call Judge Grady. She's one of my mom's sorority sisters. They play bridge every week. She's a good judge and a fair one. I knew she'd grant the order. I just forgot how well she could read me. Always could. It's your fault, you know."

Dax had been looking straight ahead, watching the road as he spoke. But he'd turned to look at her now as he pulled over to the curb in front of her building.

"What do you mean it's my fault?" Gessie sputtered.

"It's your fault you're a beautiful, intelligent, and intriguing woman. I'm crazy about you, and apparently, everyone can see it. No doubt Judge Grady will be on the phone to my mom as soon as she gets a chance."

"Oh," was all Gessie managed to say.

Dax gave her a big grin, flipped on the flashing lights, jumped out of the car and came around to open Gessie's door before she'd had time to recover from what he'd just said. She swung out her legs and accepted his offered hand. Gessie was very conscious of Dax walking beside her as he escorted her to the courtyard door. He'd never let go of her hand, and he gently pulled her against him when they stepped inside the courtyard. Before she could even think about it, he had kissed her and then spun her around with a little nudge toward her apartment door.

"I'll wait until you're inside, but I've gotta run. I want to catch Rhonda before she leaves the Autoplex for the day."

That brought Gessie out of her daze. Darn, the man. This was not like her at all. If she hadn't been so flummoxed, she might have finagled her way into going with him to the dealership. On second thought, it was probably for the best she didn't get the chance. Gessie didn't see how she could keep it from him that she was still looking into Gary's murder, if he was standing right next to her when she did it. Unfortunately, it meant she'd have to wait until the next day to go out to the dealership and talk with Rhonda herself.

Gessie was on her way up to the loft to change clothes, and to decide what she wanted to do with her evening, when there was a knock at the door. She reversed direction, went back down the stairs, and looked through the peephole. Smiling, Gessie opened the door to her friend.

"Oh good, you're already dressed up. You want to be my plus one for happy hour at Saltine?"

"Okay?"

"Come on then. It will already have started by the time we get there."

Well, what to do with her evening had been settled, even if she had no idea what she'd agreed to.

As Gessie followed Vanda to the garage, Vanda explained that she had been thinking about joining the Nashville Chamber of Commerce, and they had given her two complimentary tickets to a networking event being held at Saltine Restaurant.

"The ticket gets us each a complimentary drink and what was described as "heavy" hors d'oeuvres. I figure that's the same as a light dinner for us."

"Now, you're talking. So, is there anything I need to do to help you?"

"Not really. I'm not trying to impress them; they're trying to impress me. Supposedly there will be a mix of established and new business owners that will present me with a plethora of networking opportunities. At least that's what they told me. You can give me your take later on about the other attendees. Do you want to be yourself, or would you like to be an OTB Marketing Associate?"

OTB stood for Outside the Box and was the name Vanda used for her business. Gessie knew enough about what Vanda did to do a sales pitch for it, and they decided that would probably be better than Gessie having to explain she wasn't there as anything but a guest. Once they got that settled, Vanda looked over at her.

"Okay, now dish while I deal with this traffic. Why are you dressed up? I'm thinking that is not what you wore to take the pie over to Cole this morning. You did go to Cole's, right?"

Gessie had to take a minute to think. She couldn't believe it had been earlier that morning when she had seen Cole. So much had happened since then. Might as well start at the beginning.

"I did go to Cole's and, no, I did not wear this dress. It doesn't go with my Snoopy Vans." Getting the smile she wanted from Vanda, Gessie went on to tell her about what had happened at Cole's.

"That's awesome!" Vanda gushed when Gessie told her about Spence and Cole saying they wanted the band to record her song. "I want to hear more about that later, but I get the feeling something else happened."

"You could say that. Burton showed up."

When Vanda let out a curse, Gessie hurried to describe how Darla had seen Burton following her and had entrapped him in one of her hula hoops long enough for Gessie to see what was going on and get into the courtyard. Vanda continued to curse under her breath as Gessie described how she had stood behind the locked door with Burton pounding against it on the other side.

"I'm guessing you called Dax. Is that where the dress comes in?"

"Kind of. I texted Dax as soon as I got inside the courtyard. He showed up minutes after the other officers. Darla had called 911. Burton had heard the sirens, I guess, and he was gone before any of them got there. The officers told me I needed to get a protection order, and Dax agreed. That's where the dress came in."

She told Vanda about Dax arranging a meeting with a judge and that she'd only been back in her apartment for a few minutes before Vanda had knocked on her door.

Vanda was pulling the car into the parking lot for Saltine and easily maneuvered her Mini Cooper into a spot she'd never have been able to manage in her Audi. Vanda turned off the engine, and Gessie was reaching for the door handle when Vanda laid a hand on her arm.

"Oh no, you don't. Your voice went all soft there for a minute. You're leaving out the best part. He kissed you again, didn't he?"

Gessie just nodded her head; then, her words came out in a whisper. "He's crazy about me."

"What was that? He's what?"

"He said he was crazy about me, and everyone could see it, and it was all my fault."

"Oh boy, this is getting good. We are going to go in and do this thing, and then we're going back to your apartment, and you are going to tell me exactly what happened. Every bit of it."

Gessie didn't object. She thought it might do her some good. Her life used to be very routine. It's not like she wanted to go back to that life, but it seemed like it was currently out of control. Her emotions were all over the place, and she hadn't even had time to do any busking. She wasn't sure she missed it. She realized it was the music itself she enjoyed, not the performance part of it. Or maybe that was due to someone being interested in recording one of her songs.

As she stepped into Saltine, Gessie was almost glad to be surrounded by unfamiliar sights, sounds, and people.

CHAPTER 22

Gessie had been circulating around the edges of the gathering, sipping on her complimentary glass of wine, and trying each of the hors d'oeuvres. She found if she didn't make eye contact, she didn't have to do all that much talking. She'd only had to give the spiel on Vanda's marketing business to one man and one woman, both of which Gessie figured out were hitting on her. She handed them business cards and pointed Vanda out to them in such a way that it would have made it rude of them not to head in Vanda's direction.

She'd just popped a scrumptious hushpuppy into her mouth when she spotted Buddy Norman across the room. He was in a conversation with the woman who had taken their reservation cards and had handed them their complimentary drink tickets as she ushered them into the private area reserved for the Chamber event. The woman did not appear happy and was gesturing toward the entrance to the room. Gessie could tell Buddy was excusing himself from the group of people he had been talking to, and he turned to follow the woman.

The room was packed, but Gessie had no problem making her way around her side of the room. She arrived at the entrance slightly before Buddy and the Chamber woman and quickly turned her back, pretending to look for something in her tote as they approached.

"I'm sorry, Mr. Norman," the woman was saying. "But the restaurant and the fire department were very clear we could not exceed the space limits."

"It's fine, Judy. I'll handle it. As I'm sure you know, I have invited Miss Baxter to accompany me for several of your wonderful events. I wanted to give one of our new associates the opportunity for this occasion. There's just been a breakdown in communication. I'll handle the matter."

As soon as Buddy was out the door, Gessie turned to the woman. "Uh, I ran out of my business cards and need to go out to the car for some more. Will I be able to come back inside?"

The woman was still a little flustered, but she reached over to a small stand next to the door and handed Gessie one of the already collected reservations. "I should remember you, but just in case, take this with you."

Gessie took the card and then hurried into the main area of the restaurant, just in time to see Buddy with a hand on Rhonda Baxter's arm as he guided her out the front door. It didn't look like Rhonda was happy about leaving.

When Gessie pushed her way outside the restaurant, she could see Buddy and Rhonda standing beside a car in the parking lot. She could hear Rhonda's words from where she was standing, but she started edging a little closer.

"You owe me, Buddy. You can't just use me when it's convenient."

Buddy didn't raise his voice to the same level as Rhonda's, but he had to speak firmly enough for Rhonda to hear over her own sobbing.

"Go home, Rhonda. You're high. And keep your voice down."

Unfortunately, Rhonda did as Buddy said. Her sobbing reduced to just sniveling, and Gessie could only make out a few words. She thought she heard "police" and then "scared." Finally, she thought Rhonda said something like, "You promised you'd always take care of me, Buddy."

She didn't hear the first part of what Buddy said, but he repeated she should go home. "We'll talk about all this tomorrow."

That sounded like the end of the conversation, and Gessie turned and walked back to the front door. She quickly went back through the restaurant and found Judy right where she'd left her, standing by the maître d' stand at the entrance to the Chamber's event.

"Did you get your cards?" Judy asked pleasantly.

"Oh, silly me, they were in my tote all along. I should clean this thing out."

Judy looked like she was ready to have a bonding moment about the things women carried around in their purses. So, Gessie cut her off at the pass and said she'd better get the cards to her boss. The last thing Gessie wanted was to be standing there when Buddy Norman came back into the event. She didn't know if Buddy had seen her. Even if he did, there was no reason for him to think she had overheard his conversation with Rhonda. That's what she was telling herself, but she was also telling herself she should find Vanda and tell her they needed to leave.

Gessie spotted a flash of purple and made a beeline to where Vanda was standing with three people, one of whom was the man who had tried to hit on her earlier. Maybe she wouldn't have too much trouble convincing Vanda to leave.

"There you are, Vanda," Gessie bubbled as she approached the group. "You asked me to remind you when it was time to leave for the dinner meeting with your new client."

"Oh, Gessie, I don't know what I would do without you! Please excuse me. It's been wonderful meeting with you all. Please call if you would like to discuss marketing concepts with me."

Vanda flashed a big grin and then turned to Gessie. "What's up?"

"We need to leave. Right now. I'll explain later."

They were at the door, and Vanda was telling Judy she'd enjoyed the event and would be contacting her soon regarding membership. Another thirty seconds and they would have been out of there. Instead, she heard someone behind her.

"Excuse me."

Gessie tried to ignore the voice and gave Vanda a little nudge. But Judy was blocking their way, and her face lit up.

"Oh, Mr. Norman, can we help you? Ladies, did you get an opportunity to network with Mr. Norman. He's one of our long-time members."

Vanda and Gessie turned around, and Vanda went into business mode. She extended her hand. "It's nice to meet you, Mr. Norman. I'm Vanda Dalton with OTB Marketing, and this is my associate..."

"Miss Chapel? Right?" Buddy interrupted. "I never forget a face or a name. I believe you were in the other day to buy a car, but I was called away. Are you still in the market for one?"

Gessie could have hugged Vanda when she made a show of looking at her phone.

"I'm sorry, but we need to go, or I'm going to be late for my meeting. It was nice meeting you, Mr. Norman. Thanks again for inviting me, Judy." Then she turned to Gessie and grabbed hold of her hand, tugging her out the door.

"Sorry. Bye. Thanks," Gessie called back over her shoulder as she followed Vanda out of the restaurant.

They both did a speed-walk out of the restaurant and into the parking lot. When they reached Vanda's car, they looked at each other over the rooftop, and they both broke out laughing.

"Well, that was different," Vanda said when they were in the car. "First, thank you for saving me from that creep."

"He was hitting on you, right?"

"You, too, I take it."

"Yep, what about the woman?"

"What woman? A woman hit on you? Why didn't she hit on me?"

That made Gessie start laughing again. It was just like Vanda to be offended the woman hadn't hit on her. She was appeased only when Gessie described the woman, and Vanda decided she hadn't run into her during the gathering. Aside from the creep in the last group of people, Vanda had thought the event had been a good one, and she had made several useful contacts. She figured she'd probably join the Chamber of Commerce.

Vanda turned serious. "Now, what was the deal with Buddy Norman, Gessie. I didn't like the way he was looking at you there at the end. Why do I get the feeling you were up to something?"

Gessie wasn't laughing either when she told Vanda about the conversation she had overheard between Buddy and Rhonda.

"What do you think it means?" asked Vanda.

"Well, I guess I could look at it a couple of ways. It could be nothing more than Rhonda and Buddy have known each other for a long time, and we know from the old newspaper clippings and the commercials that she was once the woman he had on his arm. Buddy seemed to want to distance himself from her, and you can't blame him if she's always strung out on drugs."

"And what's the other way you can look at it?" prompted Vanda.

"The other way is that she had something to do with Gary's murder, and Buddy was supposed to protect her from the police. Dax said he was going out to the dealership to talk with her, and he must have upset her. Buddy put her off. He told her to go home, and he'd talk to her tomorrow."

"You need to call Dax and tell him. He can't be mad at you for overhearing something at an event you hadn't planned to go to, let alone to see Buddy and Rhonda there."

Gessie wasn't so sure about that, but she did agree that she should probably tell Dax what she had overheard. Maybe it would tie in with something he had learned, and it would get Cole off the hook once and for all.

Gessie and Vanda were just entering the courtyard from the garage, when Gessie stopped in her tracks. She could see Burton standing under the light above her apartment door.

"Go back in the garage, Gessie. I'll call 911."

"No. This has gone on long enough."

Gessie told Vanda to be ready to call 911 but to hold off.

"What are you doing here, Burton? If I call the police, you'll be arrested, and this time you'll spend a lot more time in jail."

Burton took a step away from the door.

"No. Do not come any closer. What do you want?"

"Gessie, this is crazy. You need to come home. You don't belong here. You belong to me."

Burton was agitated and was waving around what Gessie assumed was the protection order.

"Burton, do you even realize what you're saying? I do not *belong* to you. I am not a possession. I will never be what you want me to be. This is where I am now. I'm happy. I have some wonderful friends, and I have my music."

"Gessie..." Burton had taken another step.

"Stop. Go home, Burton. If you don't, I will call the police. Think about that, Burton. If you are arrested again, you could lose your job. Are you willing to ruin your life just because you didn't like it that I decided to leave?"

Gessie held her breath but knew she'd finally gotten through to Burton when he began spouting off his distaste for her and how he couldn't imagine what he'd ever seen in her.

"I hear you've lowered yourself to singing on the street for money. The gutter is where you'll most likely end up."

Gessie had made sure Burton was heading for the courtyard door and not making any move toward her. Once he was outside the door, Vanda quickly moved to it and flipped the lock. "I think we'll just keep this locked tonight. I could use a drink. You want to join me?"

Vanda opened her apartment door and gestured Gessie over to the sofa. "Make yourself comfortable. I'll get the wine. You go ahead and call Dax."

Gessie sunk into the sofa. The adrenaline was starting to ebb out of her system, and she felt completely drained. She wasn't sure how much more of this day she could take. She pulled up Dax's number on her phone.

Dax answered on the first ring. "What can I do for you, Miss Chapel?"

That made Gessie smile. "I assume you're still at work, Detective Warner."

"That would be correct. Do you have some additional information related to my case?"

"Yes, and I'll tell you about that, but I wanted to let you know Burton was here again."

All the careful wording and the polite intonation were gone.

"What? Gessie, are you okay? Did you call 911?"

"No."

"No?" Dax said, raising his voice. "You..."

"Just listen."

Gessie could almost feel Dax's agitation through the phone as she told him what had happened.

"I'm convinced he'll go home, Dax."

Dax was quiet for a minute.

"Dax?"

"Sorry, Gessie. Look, I'm not surprised you handled it yourself. It sounds like you did good. But I think I'll just go over to his hotel and see if I can give him a ride to the airport. I'll call you later."

Before Gessie could remind him she still had something to tell him about the case, she was listening to a dial tone. He did say he'd call later. So, maybe she'd still get the chance.

Gessie turned to Vanda, who had been listening to her side of the conversation. She was grinning like the Cheshire cat.

"What's that look for, Vanda?"

"You've got it bad for that guy. I'll admit I thought you and Cole were going to be a thing. The electricity between the two of you is obvious. But this is different."

"I think you're imagining things. I'm not looking for a relationship."

"Too bad. Sometimes the relationship finds you." Vanda softened her tone. "Your whole face lit up while you were talking with Dax. And that's something considering the topic of conversation."

Gessie was already confused enough, all on her own. She wasn't sure she was ready to admit to herself that what Vanda was saying was true. She gave Vanda a non-committal response. One Vanda completely ignored, but being the friend she was, she let the matter drop. Gessie stood up and grabbed her tote.

"I think I've had enough of this day, and I'm dying to get out of this dress and put on a pair of sweats. I think I'm in dire need of a music therapy session. Talk to you tomorrow?"

"Yep, it's your turn to host happy hour. I'll text you when I'm done for the day, and you can fill me in on whatever trouble it is you manage to get yourself into tomorrow."

Knowing she had every intention of trying to talk with Rhonda the next day, she didn't even bother to protest Vanda's prediction she would get into trouble. It seemed to follow her these days.

CHAPTER 23

O nce inside her apartment, Gessie lost no time doing exactly what she had said she'd do. She changed out of her dress and into her favorite pair of sweats and a t-shirt that had seen much better days. She had been pleased to find the tee because she had thought she'd left it behind in California somehow. Even worse, she had imagined it would have been just like Burton to throw it out without telling her.

Gessie couldn't help but shudder at the thought. She'd worn it one time when she was living with Burton, and he had called it a rag and insisted she take it off. Sure, the picture of Martina McBride on the front was faded, and the hem on the bottom of the shirt was fraying in places. But it was a souvenir her mother had bought her at a concert they had attended together when Gessie was sixteen. They'd had front row seats, and her mother had been just as into the concert as Gessie had been. It was a great memory, and since moving to Nashville, she'd found wearing the shirt always inspired her when she was working on a new song.

Gessie undid her chignon, shook her head back and forth, and then did a finger comb through her hair, letting it fall free. She hadn't cut it in a while, and it now fell past her shoulders. Feeling much better, Gessie padded down the stairs in bare feet. She sidetracked into the kitchen, where she grabbed a bottle of water and then set it on the dining table. She grabbed a pad of paper and a pencil and then picked up her guitar.

She already had the start of some words for a new song, but the melody that began flowing from her fingers didn't match at all. Instead, she found herself thinking of finding love when you least expected to do so. As if she had conjured him up, she got a text from Dax. She was expecting to hear from him. So, she wasn't surprised at the text. She was surprised, however, at what the text said.

"I'm at your door."

This was followed by a light knock.

Gessie hurried to the door. "Dax. Is everything okay?" Gessie asked as she opened the door.

Dax didn't answer. Gessie could feel his gaze take her in from head to toe. Gessie's heart began pounding so hard she was sure Dax could hear it. When his eyes found and held hers, there was no mistaking what he was feeling. His voice was husky when he finally spoke.

"Maybe this wasn't such a good idea."

Gessie was still rooted to the spot. She couldn't seem to say anything, and her eyes were locked with Dax's.

"Gessie, I'm about two seconds away from doing something that I don't think you're ready for. I don't want to ruin my chance with you. So, you either need to step back up a couple of steps and invite me in for coffee, or I just need to turn around and leave."

Gessie wasn't sure whether to be relieved or angry that Dax was exhibiting such self-control. But she had to admit she was struggling more than just a little bit herself. She would have liked nothing better in that moment to step into Dax's arms, knowing full well what would follow. She still had that twinge of doubt, however, that told her she didn't want to rush into anything.

"Won't you come in, Dax?" Gessie said as calmly as she could while taking two steps back. "I'll put on some coffee." She turned quickly and walked toward the kitchen. She didn't have to turn around to know that Dax had followed her into the room, and that he was watching her.

"Have a seat," she called out over her shoulder. She moved her guitar over by the sofa and then walked into the kitchen, where she took her time making the two mugs of coffee. It gave her heart time to stop racing.

She thought she had her emotions back under control when she set the two mugs of coffee down on the table. The only way to keep them that way was to steer the conversation away from anything personal.

"So, I wanted to tell you about a conversation I overheard between Buddy Norman and Rhonda Baxter."

That certainly changed the expression on Dax's face, but it wasn't the scowl Gessie had expected. It was more one of exasperation.

"Okay, we'll get to that and why you continue to ignore my request that you stay out of my investigation, but first, I want to let you know that Burton is winging his way back to California as we speak."

"He's really gone?"

"Yep, drove him to the airport myself and didn't leave until I knew the plane had taken off with him on it."

Dax told her he had driven to Burton's hotel and walked up to the front desk as the concierge was telling Burton there was a flight leaving in an hour's time, but it was doubtful Burton would be able to make it considering traffic and security. Dax had stepped in and said he could make it happen.

"Lights and sirens can come in handy," Dax quipped. "It gave me a chance to have a lovely conversation with ol' Burt. I found out he hates being called that. So, I gleefully called him that every chance I got. I impressed upon him what would happen if he ever bothered you again. I managed to refrain from dislocating his jaw, and we parted the best of friends."

Dax's words were dripping with sarcasm, but he softened his voice when he added, "You don't have to worry about him anymore, Gessie."

"Thank you, Dax."

The words might have been simple, but the fact that it was Dax reassuring her made it real. Gessie could finally put Burton behind her. Maybe she was feeling so relieved she was a little giddy. That's what she told herself anyway, when she looked across at Dax and gave a mischievous smile.

"Well, since you have so gallantly solved a problem for me, I think I'll repay you by solving your case for you."

"Whoa, whoa. Wait a minute. You should not be involved with this."

Gessie just kept smiling. "So, you don't want to know what I heard?"

"Gessie..."

"Drink your coffee, Dax." Gessie felt lighter, happier than she had in a long while. She knew most of it probably stemmed from finally having Burton out of her life. She hadn't realized just how much the toxic relationship had still been affecting her. It was good to be rid of him. She also knew a part of her happiness was due to Dax. He was probably right. She wasn't quite ready. But she had a feeling that was going to change fairly soon. She was just as motivated to get the case solved as Dax was.

"First, I didn't plan for it to happen. Vanda asked me to go with her to a Chamber of Commerce function, and there was a bit of commotion involving Buddy Norman."

Gessie had to give Dax credit, he listened very intently and didn't interrupt her as she told him about Rhonda showing up to the event uninvited and what she had overheard when Buddy had told her to go home.

"I'm guessing you shook Rhonda up when you talked with her. I think she immediately ran to Buddy, expecting him to, somehow, make your interest in her go away. When Buddy wasn't there for her after your interview, she would have been upset and became even more so when she found out he had left and taken someone else to an event she used to attend with him. I didn't get a good look at her, but from what Buddy said, she must have gotten high to get up the courage to confront him."

When Gessie finished, Dax told her the information she had given him was good, and he'd take it into account.

"Wait. You agree that Rhonda is a person of interest, don't you? Because I've been thinking about what she said. I think she killed Gary, and Buddy knows it. For some reason, I think Buddy is protecting her. Maybe for old time's sake. But I've seen the look he gave her twice now. She disgusts him. I wonder how much longer he'll protect her. Maybe she knows that at some level. Did you talk to Buddy again, too?"

Dax sighed. This time he did have a frown on his face. "Gessie, I'm serious. You need to let me do my job. I'm good at it. If it makes you feel any better, Rhonda has always been a person of interest, and so has Buddy. Just like Cole Trammel and Spence Appleby. That whole circle of friends. Add to that the people Gary came into contact with when he was an addict and those he may have encountered during his rehabilitation. I'm probably wasting my breath, but I'm going to ask you, once again, to stay out of this. Some of the people involved are not very nice. I don't want to see anything happen to you."

Dax stood up suddenly and said he had to get going.

Gessie got up and followed him to the door. Trying to keep the moment light, she said, "Give me a little more notice next time; I'll be more presentable."

Dax had his hand on the doorknob but stopped abruptly and turned back toward her. "When you opened the door, you took my breath away. It's an image I'm not even going to try to forget. The way you look tonight is perfect and sexy as hell." Then with a devilish grin, he added, "And Martina has never looked better."

With that, Dax opened the door and walked into the courtyard. He turned back one last time as Gessie stood in the doorway framed by the light from inside her apartment. "You undo me, Gessie Chapel."

Gessie watched Dax as he disappeared through the door out to 2nd Avenue.

"I undo him?" Gessie asked herself. "Who says that?" Gessie didn't know exactly what he meant by the comment, but she knew the way he said it brought a flush to her cheeks, and she felt as if she had been caressed. She smiled to herself. He liked her Martina McBride t-shirt. He just might be a keeper.

Gessie picked up the mugs from the table, took them into the kitchen, and put them into the dishwasher. She realized she was humming the melody she had been working on before Dax had shown up at her door. Dax was quickly becoming a rival for the t-shirt in the inspiration department. She was lost in the music. She began writing the notes and chords on her notepad as she played, adjusted, played the melody over and over on her guitar. When she was satisfied with what she had, she called it a night. Words were swimming around in her head, but the feelings behind them were too new, too raw to put on paper yet. It seemed too personal at the moment.

Realizing it was late, Gessie gently placed her guitar in its case and went up to bed. She wanted to be up early enough for a run in the morning and wanted to call the dealership as soon as it opened to make an appointment with Rhonda. She felt a little guilty about ignoring Dax's request for her to leave things alone. But she convinced herself, he'd be okay with it if it meant his case got solved sooner.

CHAPTER 24

Gessie got up a little later than usual, but with the mornings a little colder now, she was happier running when the sun had been up for a while. She'd discovered she didn't much like it when she could see her breath as she ran and could feel the impact the accompanying dry air had on her lungs. She'd been spoiled by the weather in California. It had been a while since she had experienced all four seasons. She'd have to adjust her run times for later in the day or start bundling up. Once winter set in, she might have to look for an alternate form of exercise until spring.

At nine o'clock on the dot, Gessie dialed the Buddy Norman Autoplex. She asked the woman who answered if Rhonda Baxter was available. The woman told her Rhonda was in, but she and the other sales personnel were all in a meeting.

"Do you think she'd be available by ten o'clock?" Gessie asked. "I was hoping to get a test drive in the new Lexus NX.

The woman assured her the meeting would be over long before that, and she would make sure Rhonda knew Gessie would be there at ten for a test drive.

She hurried to take a shower and get dressed. She wasn't trying to attract the attention of Buddy Norman this time. He was the last person she wanted to see. She decided comfort was more important than style, and she grabbed her Levis and a tunic length long-sleeved knit top. Knowing it would be easier to drive with flats, she slipped on her Allbirds Breezers.

After blow-drying her hair, she just clipped it up into a messy top knot and then applied light makeup. She wasn't trying to impress anyone today. She was on a mission.

She pulled her Coach crossbody bag off the hook on the back of the closet door and went down the stairs. She transferred everything out of her tote and into the crossbody bag, grabbed her keys, and headed out of her apartment.

As she maneuvered the Audi out of the garage, she cursed, as usual, and struggled to get out of the space without scratching her car, or somebody else's. She told herself she did need to get a new car. She wasn't just making up an excuse to try to talk with Rhonda.

The morning rush hour was over, and the drive was uneventful, giving Gessie plenty of time to plan how she was going to get Rhonda to talk about Gary's murder. The more she thought about the exchange she had overheard between Buddy and Rhonda, the more she was convinced that

Rhonda had killed Gary. The argument at the NA meeting pointed to a motive in Gessie's mind. Rejection could make someone angry enough to kill, especially if the emotions were fueled by drugs.

When Gessie reached the Autoplex, she ignored the entrance that led to the main building. She had parked in front of that building before and knew it was where Buddy's office was. She turned into the entrance for the furthest building, which featured the Lexus line of cars. As she pulled into an open spot at the far end of the building and got out of her car, a young man approached her.

"Welcome to the Buddy Norman Autoplex, where we'll drum up a deal for you."

The young man had delivered the dealership's slogan with a big smile. It dimmed considerably when Gessie told him she had an appointment with Rhonda.

"Oh, I just saw her walking toward that line of cars." He gestured toward a row of Lexus vehicles that stretched for what looked like a full city block.

Gessie had followed the gesture, and when she turned to thank the young man, he was already retreating toward the building. With no possibility of a sale for him, he had already dismissed her.

Figuring she could survey the different cars as she looked for Rhonda, Gessie started walking down the row of cars. She'd passed several of the RX models and confirmed what she'd already decided; they were bigger than what she wanted. As she reached the area with the NX models, a movement in one of the cars caught her eye.

Gessie could see Rhonda in the driver's seat of a silver NX. She was wondering if Rhonda was getting ready to drive it to the front for her. She approached the car carefully because Rhonda wasn't looking up, and she didn't want to startle her. But then it registered with Gessie what she was seeing because she had seen Burton do the same thing on occasion. Rhonda wasn't looking up because she was in the process of snorting cocaine.

"Unbelievable," Gessie said to herself, "Rhonda has to get herself high to bolster her confidence for making a sale."

Gessie wasn't sure if Rhonda being high was going to make getting information out of her easier or harder. One thing she was sure of, she wasn't going to be sitting in the passenger seat if Rhonda was driving.

As Rhonda raised her head, Gessie started to wave to get her attention. Rhonda looked right at her, then seemed to gasp. Her body began to convulse, and her head hit against the window.

Gessie ran to the car and opened the door. She had to lean against Rhonda to keep her from falling out the door. "Hold on, Rhonda, I'm going to get you some help."

Gessie managed to get her phone out of her purse and punched in 911. She told the operator who answered she was with a person who had OD'd. She gave her location, being specific that she was on the south side of the Lexus building.

She was surprised but mostly relieved when a police car pulled into the dealership entrance in under two minutes. She was still supporting Rhonda's weight so that she wouldn't tumble out of the car. So, the best Gessie could do was raise her hand and wave, hoping the police could see over the rooftop of the car next to them. It must have worked because the siren cut off, and the police car stopped directly in front of where she was standing. Two officers jumped out of the car, with one going to the trunk of the cruiser, and the other rushing to where Gessie was holding up Rhonda. She moved out of the way as the officer snapped on some gloves and took hold of Rhonda. He took one look at her and called out to his partner, "Get that Narcan over here quick, Brett."

"Do you know her name?" the officer asked Gessie as he opened a packet and handed a syringe to his partner.

"It's Rhonda. Rhonda Baxter."

Gessie stepped even further back as the two officers worked on Rhonda. They were talking loudly to Rhonda, trying to bring her around as they injected the Narcan. Gessie was close enough to see the expressions on their faces and heard them say they didn't know if one shot of Narcan was going to be enough. EMS had been dispatched at the same time as the officers, and they were hoping they'd be able to administer another dose when they got there.

The ambulance arrived moments later, and the officers seemed just as relieved to turn Rhonda over to them as Gessie had been to hand Rhonda off to the officers. Gessie

239

had been so intent on watching the EMS techs loading Rhonda into the ambulance that she hadn't noticed the group of people who had come over to see what was going on. She couldn't see the person from where she was standing. But she had no doubt the voice she was hearing belonged to Buddy Norman. That was confirmed when Buddy advised the officer he was the owner and demanded to know what was going on.

The officer turned and moved just enough that Buddy got a clear view of her. Gessie could almost see the wheels turning in his head. Still, she was surprised when he pointed at her. "What's she doing here? Did she do something to Rhonda?"

Up until this point, the officers had been treating her as a concerned citizen—one who had been at the right place at the right time for Rhonda Baxter. Now, however, the way the officers were looking at her made her think they were reconsidering their initial treatment.

One of the officers had started walking toward Gessie, when there was a chirp from another siren, and an unmarked, silver sedan pulled into the spot just vacated by the ambulance. Gessie didn't know whether she should be relieved or look for a place to hide when Detective Dax Warner popped out of the car. Dax did a slow survey of the area, and his eyes locked briefly with hers before walking to where the two officers were standing with Buddy Norman.

Gessie stood her ground and did her best to ignore what had turned into a rant by Buddy Norman, demanding to know why they weren't questioning Gessie.

As he approached the trio, Dax raised a hand and made a stopping motion and then spoke calmly but firmly to Buddy. "We'll be talking with the young woman, Mr. Norman. You can help by getting your employees and customers away from the area. We'll give you an update as soon as we determine what happened."

Buddy gave Gessie a final, hard stare and then turned to the group of people behind him. "Come on, folks, let's get back to what we were doing and let these fine officers do their job." As the group began to move, Buddy turned back to Dax. "I'll be in my office, Detective."

Buddy had spoken like he was in control and that he expected Dax to give him an update sooner rather than later.

Knowing Dax, Gessie thought it probably took all his self-control not to roll his eyes. She watched as he spoke to the two officers for a few minutes. The two officers gave her a nod and then walked back to their patrol car as Dax walked toward her. He had a frown on his face. She was expecting him to be angry with her, but she was wrong.

"Gessie, you're shivering. Let's get you into my car, and you can tell me what happened."

Dax took her gently by the arm and led her to his car. As soon as he had her seated in the passenger seat, Dax walked quickly around to the driver's side. He turned on the heat in the car and then shifted in his seat so he could face her.

Gessie figured now that they were alone, this was where the stern lecture would come in. But Dax spoke so softly, and with such concern, it was all Gessie could do not to break out in tears. The horror of what she had just witnessed was coming back to her.

"Are you okay, Gessie? Can you tell me what happened?"

Dax had reached across and taken Gessie's hands in his and was waiting patiently for her to begin. The heater was nice, but it was the warmth from Dax's hands that finally stopped her shivering.

"I came to look for a new car. Really," she added, and Dax gave a slight roll of his eyes. That made her smile and brought her almost back to normal. "Okay, I admit I could have looked for a car somewhere else, but I had seen one I liked the first time I was here. I figured what would it hurt if I took a test drive with Rhonda and see if I could get her talking about Gary."

Gessie paused for a minute. She was getting distracted. As he held her hands, Dax was gently caressing the back of one of them. What should have been a soothing gesture was causing a much different reaction for Gessie. She loved the feel of his hands, and she was starting to imagine them caressing other parts of her body. She knew she was probably blushing, and she pulled her hands away from Dax, clinching them together in front of her.

Dax hadn't missed the look or the blush on Gessie's face. Gessie thought she saw his lips twitch, but thankfully he didn't make a comment about the effect just his touch had on her. He leaned back a bit and then asked her to go on.

"I think Rhonda was about to pull out a car for me for the test drive. I'm sure she didn't expect me to be walking down the row of cars looking for her. I can't imagine she would have been snorting cocaine if she thought I was going to be coming up on her. Then again, some people think it's no big deal if other people see them. Like it's cool or something." Gessie couldn't help but picture Burton standing in front of her and proclaiming arrogantly that she was somehow inferior and ignorant because she wasn't even willing to try the drug. Again, Dax was watching her intently, but he didn't rush her story.

"Anyway, when I was almost to the car, I could tell what she was doing. I swear, when she looked up, there was a look of shock on her face. She saw me, but I don't know if she tried to say anything or not. She immediately began convulsing. I think she hit her head pretty hard against the driver's side window."

Gessie finished by describing how she had opened the car door and then had stayed there, sort of keeping Rhonda propped up until the police arrived.

"Her lips had a blue tinge to them, and she was kind of gurgling."

"If she was snorting cocaine, it sounds like it was laced with fentanyl. That can be a deadly mix if someone isn't used to the fentanyl. Sometimes it's deadly even if they are used to it. Most of the people who have been revived from a cocaine-fentanyl overdose had no idea they were taking anything other than their normal cocaine hit."

"Was Gary Armbruster's overdose related to fentanyl, too?" Gessie asked.

Dax was nodding and seemed to be thinking.

"Gessie, are you okay now? I promised the officers I'd have you go over to the Midtown Precinct and give them an official statement. I've got to go talk with Buddy Norman and then go to the hospital. I haven't heard anything to the contrary, so I'm hoping they're having some success treating Rhonda, and she'll be able to talk to me. If she thinks someone has done this to her, maybe she'll open up about everything."

Gessie said she was fine and would go to the precinct right away.

"Dax," Gessie said as he began walking with her to her car, "did you notice Buddy was making a big fuss about me, but he never asked how Rhonda was? He didn't ask what hospital they were taking her to. It was like he expected her not to make it."

"Yeah, I noticed, Gessie. Believe me, Buddy Norman and I are going to have a conversation. I doubt it's the one he's expecting. He seems to believe his standing in the community means everyone is in awe of him. There's something off about the guy, and I don't like that he seems to be focused on you. Please stay as far away from him as possible. Can you do that for me?"

When Gessie said she wanted to be nowhere near Buddy Norman again—ever, Dax seemed to relax just a bit. He waited until Gessie was in the driver's seat of her Audi and then patted the rooftop above her head. "Stay safe."

Gessie backed out of her parking spot and watched as Dax continued toward the middle building and Buddy's office.

CHAPTER 25

It didn't take her as long as she'd expected to have her statement taken. Dax must have assured the responding officers that Buddy's ranting was just posturing because they didn't question her version of what had happened. Gessie signed her statement, and when she got into her car, she fully intended to go back home. But as she neared 21st Avenue, she began to see signs for the Vanderbilt University's Emergency Center. She had heard the EMS team tell the officers that's where they were taking Rhonda. On a whim, she followed the signs and pulled into the parking garage directly across from the Emergency entrance. She felt kind of sad for Rhonda and was compelled to see if she was going to be alright.

Gessie found a parking spot on the second tier and took the stairs down to the street level. As she started to cross the street, she saw the back of a man just walking through the emergency building entrance. She was sure it was Buddy Norman. She felt goosebumps going up her arm. She couldn't say why, but she was uneasy seeing Buddy entering the building. She hurried to follow him.

A receptionist looked up as she entered, but Gessie acted like she belonged there and pointed toward where she had just seen Buddy heading down a nearby hallway.

"I'm with him."

Gessie rushed to the hallway and saw Buddy talking to someone in hospital scrubs. Buddy nodded to the person and then disappeared to the right through a set of doors the led into what Gessie assumed was another hallway. It had worked before. So, she decided to go with it again.

"I'm with Buddy Norman. For Rhonda Baxter?" Gessie had hurried up to the man she assumed was a nurse or orderly of some kind and tried to sound a little out of breath as she gestured toward where the man had just sent Buddy. He barely gave her a look and motioned toward the set of doors.

"Through there. Third observation room on the left."

Gessie was a bit surprised she hadn't been challenged about entering the area. She'd always heard only one visitor at a time was allowed in to see a critical patient. Of course, maybe Rhonda wasn't critical. The man had said Rhonda was in an observation room, not intensive care. Maybe she just watched too much drama on TV, and it had nothing to do with the real world. The nurse or orderly, whichever he was, looked haggard. Maybe it had just been that kind of day for him, and he didn't have the energy to argue with anyone at the moment. Whatever the case, Gessie was just glad no one was there to stop her from following Buddy into Rhonda's room. She just didn't have a good feeling about Buddy being there.

The observation rooms were kind of a misnomer. They were more like a cubicle with a curtain for a door. The curtains were closed on all the rooms. So, that didn't send up an alarm with Gessie. What did send up an alarm was what she saw when she drew the curtain to Rhonda's room aside.

Buddy Norman was in the process of removing the oxygen mask that had been covering Rhonda's nose and mouth.

"Hey!" Gessie shouted, followed immediately by, "Help!"

Buddy whirled around, "You!"

Gessie could hear footsteps running, and Buddy must have heard them, too. He shoved her out of the way as he ran out of the room. Gessie's arms flailed as she fell backward. She landed hard on her butt and watched helplessly as Buddy disappeared through a doorway with an Exit sign overhead.

Someone was asking Gessie if she was okay and was trying to help her up off the floor.

"I'm fine. Rhonda. Check Rhonda," Gessie insisted.

The nurse immediately went into Rhonda's room. She came back to Gessie a few minutes later, and they were joined by a man who had an ID badge indicating he was hospital security.

"Miss Baxter is fine. As for you, that was a pretty hard fall. Are you sure you don't want to be checked out?"

"I'm sure I'm going to be very sore, but I'm fine. Thank you."

The nurse gave Gessie a little frown but didn't argue any further, instead she motioned to the security guy. "This is Campbell Morgan, the head of hospital security."

"Mr. Morgan, I was coming down the hall when I saw this young woman fall to the floor as a man ran out of Miss Baxter's room."

"Can you tell us what happened, Miss...?"

"Chapel. Gessie Chapel."

Gessie had just gotten her name out when footsteps could be heard coming from behind her. There was no mistaking who was approaching the group as soon as she heard her name.

"Gessie?"

As Gessie turned, she saw Dax doing his detective thing. He was taking in everything around him. He gave Gessie a pointed look but didn't say anything to her. Instead, he spoke to Campbell Morgan.

"How are you doing, Camp? What's going on?"

"Been a while, Dax. We've had a commotion of some kind. I don't believe in coincidence, so I'm guessing you showing up means whatever happened is related to a case you're working. This young lady was involved. I take it you two know each other?"

"Yes."

Although everyone was now looking at her, Gessie directed her comments to Dax. "It was Buddy. He had his hand on Rhonda's oxygen mask. I was afraid he was trying to kill her. I shouted for help. He shoved me out of the way and ran."

Gessie didn't miss the anger that flashed briefly in Dax's eyes when she said Buddy had shoved her, but his voice was controlled when he looked away from Gessie and asked the nurse about Rhonda's status.

"The oxygen mask was askew when I checked on Miss Baxter. But she remains stable. The second dose of naloxone seems to have worked. We'll keep her under observation to make sure she doesn't experience any after-effects."

"Can I talk with her?" Dax asked.

"Her body has had a shock and needs time to recover. Let's give the oxygen and the IV a little more time. If you'll give me your information, I'll call you the moment she is strong enough to talk. I'm Beverly, by the way."

Dax nodded and then turned to Campbell Morgan. "Camp, I think we need to take some precautions here. I'm going to have an officer assigned to guard Miss Baxter. Until he gets here, I'd appreciate it if you could alert the appropriate staff to limit access to hospital personnel only."

Beverly and Campbell nodded and began to walk away, leaving Gessie alone with Dax.

"Gessie, what were you doing here? I'm beginning to feel like a broken record, repeating the same thing over and over again. Don't answer now. I need to make some calls and get some things set in motion. Let's walk to where you're parked, and when I'm off the phone, we can have a nice chat."

Gessie didn't miss Dax's exasperation and the touch of sarcasm as he talked with her. Mostly because she knew he had a right to be upset with her.

As soon as they had exited the building, Dax began making calls. She half-listened as he requested the guard for Rhonda's room and put out an all-points bulletin to locate Buddy Norman and bring him in for questioning regarding an assault at University Hospital. Her mind was working through her belief that things in the universe were all connected. It was that whole butterfly effect thing where the flapping of a butterfly's wings in one part of the world could cause a hurricane in another part. She also thought the same theory was responsible for times when individuals came together in some kind of weird way. Like when you meet someone you never knew before, and suddenly, events conspire so that the person becomes part of your universe. Sometimes they stayed in that universe to become friends or more. Other times it just seemed like they appeared in the same places you did. Perhaps they always had, and you just began noticing them. But then why did they seem to fall out of that universe for no apparent reason.

Her meeting Cole Trammel brought not only Cole but a whole lot of people into her universe. She had to admit she was responsible for some of the subsequent events. But it was by chance that Cole had walked by when she was busking on the street, and it was by chance she found out who he was when Vanda took her to The Stage. It was by chance that she was jogging at the same time Cole discovered his friend's body. That chance occurrence led to her meeting Dax. It was by chance she had been at the Chamber of Commerce meeting where she heard Buddy and Rhonda argue. And while some would say it was inevitable, Gessie still thought the butterfly was madly flapping its wings to influence the timing that had Buddy, Gessie, and Dax appearing within minutes of each other at the hospital to see Rhonda.

Gessie was brought out of her thoughts by Dax calling her name. He had said it a little too loud. So, she figured it must not have been the first time he'd tried to get her attention.

"Sorry, I was lost in thought."

Knowing Dax wanted an explanation for why she was at the hospital, she told him she just wanted to know how Rhonda was doing. Seeing Rhonda overdose had affected her more than she'd thought, and she hoped it would help somehow if she could make sure Rhonda was going to be alright. She went through her story again for Dax about the feeling she had gotten when she had seen Buddy walking into the hospital.

"Come here," Dax said softly as he pulled Gessie into his arms.

Gessie didn't realize how much she needed the hug, and she couldn't help the tears that began to fall as she pictured Rhonda helpless in the car and then Buddy's enraged face when she'd interrupted him standing over Rhonda at the hospital.

She didn't know how long they stood there like that, neither of them saying a word. Gessie finally relaxed, and as they stepped apart, Gessie looked at Dax's eyes. They were filled with concern.

"Thanks, I needed that," Gessie smiled.

"I'm just glad you're okay. I've got to admit you've got some good instincts. They've been spot on in this case. But I don't like that your instincts keep putting you in situations where you can get hurt. Where you *have* been hurt. It's hard for me to keep focused when I'm worrying about you."

It made Gessie feel a little guilty that Dax was more worried about her than angry. "Okay, I'll go home, I promise. Before I go, can you tell me what happened when you talked with Buddy?"

Dax sighed. "I shouldn't tell you, but it would probably make things easier and maybe help you keep your promise this time."

Dax told her that Buddy had admitted he knew Rhonda sometimes took drugs, but he thought she'd had it under control. He'd also accused Gessie of stalking both him and Rhonda and said he thought she had some crazy attraction to him and saw Rhonda as a threat.

Gessie couldn't help it, she interrupted. "You. Are. Kidding me. What an arrogant, delusional…"

"Oh yeah, he's all of that. In fact, I want to warn you. From what you described, I can see Buddy spinning a tale that he ran because he was afraid of you."

Gessie was practically sputtering. It took her a minute to get her mind wrapped around what Dax was saying. When it sunk in, she wondered if Dax was right.

"He might have to feign a bit of embarrassment if he ran and left Rhonda in my clutches. Unfortunately, I can see him doing that as well."

"I'm hoping Rhonda will come around so that I can talk with her before questioning Buddy. Hopefully, that would give me some ammunition to counteract Buddy's theatrics."

Gessie felt almost numb, and Dax asked if she was sure she was okay to drive home. Gessie assured him she was and got into her car. As she turned on the engine and put the car into gear, Dax patted the roof of the car and then stepped aside to watch as she drove out of the garage. She'd asked him about the pat on the roof the first time he had done it, and he had told her it was kind of a law enforcement thing. It meant the person in the car was special, and the person patting the roof wanted them to be safe. Sometimes the words accompanied the pat, other times not. Either way, Gessie had to admit, she did feel special and protected. She was going to try very hard to keep her promise to stay out of things and let Dax do his job.

When she got back home, she took off her clothes and fell into bed, face first. It had to be face first because the bruise on her backside was already apparent, and it was very sore, even against a soft mattress. She was still tender from when Burton had shoved her. So, the added shove from Buddy assured she was likely to be hurting for some time. This was another trend she hoped wasn't going to continue. She tried to get comfortable so she could catch a little nap. She figured she was going to need all her strength later when she explained her latest foray into chaos theory to Vanda.

CHAPTER 26

W hen Friday rolled around, Gessie's world had changed. She'd walked into Spence's music store just as Cole was saying good-bye to a beautiful redhead. It was obvious they were more than friends. Cole spotted Gessie and was just a bit sheepish as he introduced her to the young woman.

"Gessie Chapel, this is Lauren Armbruster. She's Gary's cousin." Gessie was only slightly surprised at herself when she realized she wasn't at all upset at seeing the young woman with Cole. She was happy for him. He looked so much better now that Gary's murder was no longer hanging over his head. The lawsuit had been dropped, and Gary's family had made peace with Cole. That must have included Lauren, and she suspected a prior relationship had been rekindled in the process. Gessie decided she probably would have looked sheepish too if she had walked in with Dax on her arm. She figured Cole wouldn't have been any more upset to see her with Dax than she was to see him with Lauren.

There might still be a little spark there, and maybe there would always be a special connection between the two of them. But Gessie knew it would just be as friends. That was probably for the best anyway since it looked like she might be writing more songs in the future for the Cole Trammel Band.

Before Lauren left, she smiled brightly at Gessie. "I lucked out and got the last piece of that marvelous pie you made. I hope you'll give me the recipe."

"Well, it's an old family recipe." Gessie paused as if she was considering refusing the request. Then she added, "Lucky for you, the family is named Crocker. The only things I can think of that might have made it different from Betty's recipe was the fresh peaches from the Farmers' Market and the Sugar in the Raw sprinkled on top."

Lauren laughed and then turned serious. "Thank you, Gessie. You're a good friend, and since Cole wants to stay in your good graces, I told him he needed to get that special pie pan back to you. What a hoot that is. I brought it here for you, and Spence put it in an office somewhere. So, be sure he gets it for you before you leave. But watch out, he seems to think it's like a coffee refill, and if he hands it back to you, you'll return it with another pie inside."

"That's not how it works?" Spence asked as he joined them. "Oh well, a guy's gotta try. Come on, Gessie, I'll take you back to the studio."

Later, as she'd finished singing "No Time Like the Present," she had to keep from pinching herself to see if she was in a dream. Not only had the band liked the song, they had wanted her to stay and work with them to brainstorm ideas for the band's arrangement of the song. She found out she agreed with Cole's earlier assessment when he had told her Matt was savant-like at arrangements. She had sent an advance copy of the lyrics and melody to the band, and Matt already had a good start on an arrangement. But that didn't stop him from getting input and ideas from the rest of the band. Gessie was beyond thrilled they had included her as they talked lead-ins, harmonies, and instrumental breaks. It was all pretty heady stuff for Gessie.

When the initial arrangement had been agreed upon, she listened as the band began playing their version of her song. They started by going through the melody, with Trey picking up the rhythm on the drums. The third time through, Cole began to sing the lyrics with Spence and Matt testing out harmonies. The song was taking shape, and the band voted unanimously to include it on their upcoming album. Spence made sure he handed her the Pi plate and said he would be getting in touch with her to work out a contract for her song. Plus, the band had made it clear they would like to hear other songs she had written. Old or new.

Gessie was practically floating when she left the recording studio. As she walked the few blocks from Spence's store to her apartment, she texted Dax to let him know she was on her way home. His return text let her know he'd be there in an hour.

When Gessie got home, her feeling of euphoria was mixed by just a touch of anxiety. This would be her first date with Dax. She'd spoken to him but hadn't seen him since that day at the hospital.

Things had happened fairly quickly after she left the hospital. Rhonda had been feeling well enough to talk later that evening, and she had held nothing back. She'd told Dax that Buddy was the one who supplied her with cocaine. Rhonda had no idea the batch she had taken that day was laced with fentanyl, but was convinced Buddy would have known. Rhonda was mad and scared at the same time. Dax managed to get her to tell him she had injected Gary with the drugs that killed him.

She had been angry that Gary didn't want to see her anymore because she was still using. She'd gone crying to Buddy, and he'd come up with an idea to get Gary hooked back on drugs. When he'd been commiserating with her, Buddy had told Rhonda he wasn't happy Gary was dropping the lawsuit against Cole. She said Buddy hated Cole, and he had been the one to talk Gary into the lawsuit in the first place. At the time, Gary would go along with anything to buy drugs with the money Buddy gave him. Once he was clean and saw how Buddy had manipulated him, he told Buddy the same thing he had told Rhonda. He didn't want Buddy anywhere in his life, and he was going to make things right with Cole.

Rhonda said Buddy was furious, and he told her his plan would get back at Gary for both of them. Dax was convinced Rhonda thought she was just shooting Gary up with enough heroin to get him hooked on it. She had called Gary up that night and convinced him that she was in crisis and needed his help. She'd had him meet her by the train station and, at some point, got him to drink a bottle of water she had brought that was laced with something Buddy had told her would knock Gary out so that she'd have no trouble injecting the heroin.

Just like the cocaine Buddy had given Rhonda, the heroin had been mixed with fentanyl, making it what was referred to as a "hotshot." Gary never had a chance. Buddy had supplied the hotshot to Rhonda, and she was certain Buddy had done so purposely.

Dax had believed Rhonda when she said she didn't know Buddy had intended to kill Gary all along. She had been so upset when he died; she had gone to Buddy for more and more cocaine. She'd needed to stay high just to function. Rhonda and Buddy had started arguing more and more as well, and Dax figured Buddy had tried to eliminate the possibility Rhonda would put all the pieces together and turn on him.

They'd found Buddy the next day, hiding out on his boat at the marina on Percy Priest Lake. He'd said he was just taking a much-needed break from all the stress he'd been under. Not surprisingly, he feigned complete innocence and shock at the story he claimed Rhonda had concocted to protect herself. He even worked up some tears, saying he had lost two old friends because of what one had done to the other. His version of what happened at the hospital went pretty much as Dax had predicted—Buddy tried to direct suspicion to Gessie. Buddy claimed he was caressing Rhonda's face, and he must have accidentally hit the oxygen mask when Gessie scared him. He was just trying to get away from a crazy stalker.

Buddy's lawyer was successful in getting him released, claiming everything they had on Buddy was circumstantial and based on the word of a drug addict and a street person. The street person he referenced was Gessie. Apparently, the lawyer had the same opinion of buskers as good ol' Burton. Gessie had gotten the impression from Dax that he'd used every bit of his self-control not to punch the lawyer in the face.

Although Buddy had been released, Dax had no doubt he'd eventually be charged. Rhonda had given them a couple of names for the dealers Buddy might have gotten the drugs from. Vice was going to track the dealers down and put some pressure on them for the information. Rhonda wasn't able to post her bail and was just as happy not to be anywhere Buddy could get at her. She figured, if nothing else, it was a forced rehab.

Dax was confident that a rehabilitated Rhonda would make an excellent witness, and it was just a matter of time before Buddy was made to pay for what he'd done. In the meantime, Dax had put the word out on Buddy. If he did a rolling stop, was 1 mile over the limit, or didn't signal a turn, he was going to find himself with a ticket. He wanted Buddy to know he was being watched.

There was a knock on Gessie's door. When she opened the door, Dax didn't say hello. Instead, he said, "Fair warning, Gessie Chapel, from now on, I'm not holding anything back."

"Well, who's asking you to?" Gessie quipped as she leaped toward him. She jumped up, wrapped her legs around his waist, and clasped her hands behind his head. If the move surprised him, he didn't show it. Dax caught her as if this was the way Gessie greeted him every day. He held onto her tightly and crushed his lips against hers.

The kiss was intense and ended only because they both needed to take a breath.

"Well, now that that's settled," Gessie teased, "I think you promised to help me pick out a new car."

"On one condition," Dax answered. "We're not going anywhere near the Buddy Norman Autoplex."

* * *

Gessie ended up with a bright red Jeep Wrangler. Like many other things in her life, she was discovering what she truly liked. A luxury car wasn't one of them. She and Dax had already made plans to strip off the doors and top and go off-roading as soon as the weather got nice enough in the spring.

She also learned a little more about Dax. She found out he was 38, had a sister and a brother, and an assortment of nieces and nephews. His mother was an accountant, and his father was a partner in a prominent Nashville law firm. Dax had started out on a path to follow in his father's footsteps and had a Law Degree from Yale to prove it. But the degree included a hefty load of criminal justice coursework because Dax had decided about six months into his freshman year that he'd rather be a police officer than a lawyer.

He had a condo only blocks away from the house he grew up in, and he and his family were a close-knit bunch. Dax had been amused by all her questions, except for the ones about his ex-wife. He emphasized his marriage to Andrea (and woe be it to the person who didn't pronounce it as AWN dree AH) had been a mistake. According to Dax, his family met the news of their divorce with a mixture of relief and outright cheers. He assured Gessie there was no need for her to be anxious about joining his family for Thanksgiving and that everyone would love her.

"Thanks to Andrea, that bar is set incredibly low," Dax had teased her. She'd gotten him back for that comment when she told him her father was a national and state archery champion using a recurve bow, and couldn't wait to take Dax out to the range at Christmas.

The other big thing in Gessie's life was she was no longer busking. She still loved to sing, but she no longer felt the need to perform. When she'd heard the Cole Trammel Band singing her song, she knew it was the songwriting she loved. She still hadn't been able to put into words the pleasure and excitement she had felt when she heard her music performed by someone else. Vanda had helped Gessie set up a presence on the web, and she'd already gotten a couple of calls from artists wanting to talk with her about writing a song for them.

The Cole Trammel Band had just released their new album, and "No Time Like the Present" was rising in the country charts.

Like the words in her song said, she'd known the time had come when she needed to take a chance on herself if she was ever going to be happy. She'd taken that chance, and she'd won. She was at a perfect time and place in her life and couldn't wait to see what the next day would bring.

A Note from the Author

If you want to contact me or would like information about previous and upcoming books, check out my website: www.gertnermedia.com